SERGE PEY

The Treasure of the Spanish Civil War

Translated from French by
Donald Nicholson-Smith

archipelago books

Library of Congress Cataloging-in-Publication Data:
Names: Pey, Serge, 1950- author. | Nicholson-Smith, Donald, translator.
Title: The treasure of the Spanish Civil War / Serge Pey ; translated from
French by Donald Nicholson-Smith.
Description: First Archipelago Books edition. | Brooklyn, NY : Archipelago
Books, 2020. | "Originally published in the French as Le Trésor de la
guerre d'Espagne by Zulma, 2011"--Title page verso. |
Identifiers: LCCN 2019051644 (print) | LCCN 2019051645 (ebook) | ISBN
9781939810540 (paperback) | ISBN 9781939810557 (ebook)
Subjects: LCSH: Pey, Serge, 1950---Translations into English. | Spain--History--Civil War,
1936-1939--Refugees--Fiction. | Political refugees--France--Fiction.
Classification: LCC PQ2676.E878 A2 2020 (print) | LCC PQ2676.E878 (ebook)
| DDC 843/.914--dc23

Archipelago Books
232 3rd Street #A111
Brooklyn, NY 11215
www.archipelagobooks.org

Distributed by Penguin Random House
www.penguinrandomhouse.com

Cover art: Camp d'Argelès-sur-Mer, November 1940, Dr. Alec Cramer
Cover design: Zoe Guttenplan

This work was made possible by the New York State Council on the Arts
with the support of Governor Andrew M. Cuomo and the New York State Legislature.

This work received support from the French Ministry of Foreign Affairs and the
Cultural Services of the French Embassy in the United State through their
publishing assistance program.

Archipelago Books also gratefully acknowledges the generous support from Lannan
Foundation, Nimick Forbesway Foundation, the Carl Lesnor Foundation, the National
Endowment for the Arts, and the New York City Department of Cultural Affairs.

PRINTED IN THE UNITED STATES OF AMERICA

TRANSLATOR'S ACKNOWLEDGMENTS

As so many times before, I am indebted to Mia Nadezhda Rublowska for all kinds of support, and most especially for her merciless reading of this translation against the French. John Simmons and Richard White kindly offered me guidance on the game of chess. Great thanks too, of course, to Jill Schoolman and all at Archipelago Books.

I should like to dedicate this translation to A. Roa, an anarchist veteran of the Spanish Civil War to whom I broke a promise, very many years ago, to translate his memoir of *La Retirada* and of his sojourn in a French prison camp.

D. N.-S.

Contents

There is a mean in things: in a word, there are definite bounds
beyond and short of which what is right cannot exist.

Horace, Satires, Book I, 1, 106-7

The Treasure of the
Spanish Civil War

An Execution

THERE WERE FOUR of them at the entrance to the field. Then another one appeared behind the shed. Five now. The boy saw birds scared up from the bushes. Yet another one, rifle in hand. Six. The boy heard a horse whinnying and a bird flapping off behind a boulder. Then he saw the *guardia civil* corporal pointing them out to the other five with his cord riding-crop. Slowly the mounted guards surrounded the man and the boy.

"Are you the spitter?"

The man did not reply. He simply spat straight ahead, between the horse's legs, without lowering his head.

"You have six hours to leave this property and you won't be warned again."

The man spat for a second time between the legs of the horse, which sidestepped and reared at its own shadow. The corporal drew his revolver and, trembling, pointed it at the man's head. The man still did not look down. Then the guard, pulling his horse to the side, took aim at a little black pig that the boy and the man were fattening up for the feast days. The pig's head exploded from the impact of the shot and its body rolled soundlessly onto its side. Despite the detonation the man's gaze did not waver and he spat yet again between the horse's legs. The man had spoken.

—

3

"We'll get you soon, spitter! You'll end up like that pig and then you can go spit in hell!" said the corporal before disappearing with the other riders in a cloud of dust.

The boy watched an eagle wheeling in the sky. As though harnessed to an invisible noria, the majestic bird drew all the sunshine towards the two of them where they stood amidst shadows. The boy would remember this. The man kept silent for a long while, observing the eagle as it turned towards the mountain, perhaps to check its work and draw the sun to another valley. At last the man turned and spoke to the boy.

"Give me your knife."

The man gutted the piglet and wrapped it in leaves, then dug a hole and lit a fire in it with dry wood. When he had glowing embers he placed the animal's spread-eagled carcass on them and covered it with soil. The boy and the man had been collecting stones all morning without exchanging a single word when the boy suddenly came upon a snail's glistening shell under an old tree stump. It was glossy and yellow. A bluish spiral wound around it up to the gaping hole that once contained and protected the creature's body. The boy picked up the shell and showed it to the man.

"I found a shell."

"Keep it, kid," the man replied. "They say that shells bring good luck because they hold the voices of the departed."

The boy thought to himself that it would soon be midday.

And indeed the man pointed out the shortening shadows as they climbed the mountainside and shrank little by little. By the time the pig was ready the sun was casting no shadows.

The boy was crouched by the spring filling their canteen when he saw a flock of birds rise suddenly from a bush. Further off, the noise of a waterfall had abruptly become the only sound. Then he sensed them, up above, with their horses. He heard a man's voice yelling words he did not understand. Three shots rang out, followed by a fourth. For a brief moment the silence in the boy's chest was broken and the roar of the waterfall was deafening.

A horseman had asked, "Where's the kid?"

A rasping voice answered, "Go and see, and take care of him. He must be by the stream. You, set fire to the hut and the chicken coop."

The boy dragged himself in among an old oak tree's roots which, as they wound between rocks, had created a niche he had discovered earlier while trailing a fox. This hideaway was exactly the right size for him. He crawled backwards into the burrow and pulled a branch across the entrance to conceal it. Then he let himself slip down to the point where the narrow passageway made a right-angled turn and continued underneath a boulder.

Sweat trickled into the boy's eyes and for a moment he stopped breathing. The sound of his heart filled the whole den. He felt as though he no longer had any heart and that the whole universe was a vast throbbing.

The guard came down to the spring. The boy knew that he was inspecting the canteen that he had left behind and the wine bottle tinkling like a bell under the stream of water. The horse came close, passed above the rocks, then returned and halted by the branches that concealed his hiding place. The guard knew the boy was in there. He sensed the boy's presence. He was a hunter, honed like a knife, well used to tracking every kind of game, man or beast. The boy pictured him flaring his nostrils and deeply inhaling the scents of the forest as he scanned the trees without turning his head.

"What are you doing?" came the far-off voice of the corporal. "Did you find him?"

The guard guided his horse around the rocks. The boy heard him dismount. The sound of his boots came nearer, then he was pulling aside a few branches just above the hidey-hole. The guard knew that the boy was not far away. Suddenly his voice came, distant: "I know you're there. You can come out. I won't kill you."

The boy knew that the guard had not seen him, because he was speaking from the other side of the rocks. The guard was lying to gain his trust and then shoot him. The boy was behind the guard and very careful not to make the slightest movement for fear of causing stones to topple.

"Come out of your hole. You can't stay in there all day."

From the silence that followed the boy realized that the guard had spotted the hole. The guard knew that the boy was down inside, crouched underground. But he could not enter the boy's hiding-place because the passage was too narrow, so all he could do was fire blindly down the hole in hopes of hitting him. The boy told himself that he had a chance of surviving, for he was at the elbow-bend in the burrow behind another rock. The boy sensed that the guard now had his rifle pointing at the entrance and was about to fire.

"Come on. I'm not going to hurt you."

A stone tumbled by the boy's shoulder. It was at that moment that the guard fired wildly into the den. The bullets passed close to the boy without hitting him and grazed the rock against which he was leaning. He remained motionless, burying his face in the earth. Then the voice of the corporal resounded again.

"Come on back. Forget it. You got him. It's late already."

The guard waited for a moment. The boy heard him reload his gun and then depart on foot, leading his horse. The boy did not budge.

The boy stayed where he was, underground, for several hours. Nightfall approached. At long last the horses left, hooves resounding dully on the stones on the far side of the hill. The guards had

—

7

been waiting to see whether he might emerge, because there were to be no witnesses able to identify them. They were certain now that the boy was dead. But the boy stayed in his crevice, perfectly still, until he heard a bird begin singing once more. It was true that the boy was dead. His hand had swollen up and taken the form of a snail. His fingers had turned into slimy tentacles twisting this way and that. First the boy saw the pig that the man had roasted spread out on the ground. Then it was the dead body of a snail with its eyes open and a stone still clasped in its hands. The man too had turned into a snail. He too had fingers that waved like snail's tentacles. One by one they separated from his hands and started crawling along the ground like little translucent snakes.

The boy did not weep. He took his knife and began scraping beneath a rock. As he removed earth he found stones that he tossed behind him. When the hole was big enough he pulled over the man's body, which suddenly began to resemble an enormous glob of spittle. It had neither head nor hands and the torso was all viscous and soft. The boy took the man's wallet and knife, which were also covered with drool. He removed his leather jacket and belt and rolled him in a blanket. He left him his pack of cigarettes so that he could carry on smoking underground, even though his mouth had disappeared.

The boy gently slid the body into the hole he had made. He thought to himself that in this way the man's ghost would continue to take care of the field. Using his feet, he heaped up pebbles and arranged a circle of white ones roughly above the man's heart. Then he heard a yell. It was his own voice.

The morning sun dazzled him as he stood before the open door of the hut. The boy's mouth was full of phlegm and the snail shell was intact on the wine drum that he used as a table. A shadow raced across the mountainside: in the sky the eagle, with its invisible leash, was now drawing part of the sunlight to the other side of the valley, wrenching trees one by one from the rocks that the storms of the night had scattered across the mountain.

The boy picked up the empty shell and spat into it, several times, as though to bring it to life. He wanted a snail to be born from his saliva. Then he took his knife and made a little hole under a stone to slip the shell into. In the sky the eagle had now drawn away all the sun and the mountain was following it too. The boy cried out to them to wait for him, because he did not want to be alone. The boy told himself that he was with the man on the edge of that abyss, that he was dangling from the line of the horizon like a hanged man who, when the rope broke, would fall back into his own body.

The Washing and
the Clothes Line

THE NEIGHBORS THOUGHT my mother was crazy. How to explain that she sometimes put her washing on the line, sometimes in the field, sometimes on the grass, and sometimes even hung it from the branches of trees? What sense did it make that she would often lay it in the shade or in the windiest spot weighted down by large stones like the punctuation marks of some secret message?

On this morning my mother had taken the flowerpots outside because the sun was back. The same sun that disappeared at times behind the sun and that we would look for all over the house, in the dust, under the bed, in a book open at a ripped page, or beneath a mislaid shoe.

Beginning the day meant following a strict ritual. The first thing was the search for fire. Moment by moment, the great kindler, the sun, prepared the celebration of noon. There were days that began like night. We heard red owls hooting, bells ringing in places unknown, shutters slamming, even songs of freedom from the depths of cellars. But this time it was daytime in the day because it had already been daytime in the night.

My mother had taken the flowers outside as if to give the

—

horizon permission to stretch out, because the *tramuntana* had blown very hard and now calm reigned like a bird on a branch. By bringing the flowers in their pots from their sheltered spot in the hallway my mother was telling the sun it was time to rise.

I learned my letters as I ate my alphabet soup. Tiny letters, without much meaning. For her part, my mother read the earth, because marks on the ground were the writing of the night. From those signs, outside the house, she knew that a fox had passed by along the road, or a dog, or a bicycle. So well did she read marks on the ground that I thought she must come from the future. Sometimes she would point out a flight of birds at a place in the sky that the birds had yet to reach.

Flowers and cats were my mother's vowels. In hanging out her washing she wrote consonants that filled the world with sound. With our sheets and shirts she dictated sentences that only heaven could understand. Through the window I saw my pants, a script signaling to trucks on the main road and to unknown shepherds by their fires.

On this morning my mother seemed to be singing for an illiterate god belching forth cries like vowels. Everything was decreed: the cawing of a crow, the whine of a knife-grinder at work, a lost airplane, a crate full of guns, the voice of a white cloud altering its ephemeral aspect. This morning in particular my mother had taken the washing down from the clothes line and spread it out on the grass before going off to light a fire at the far end of the field.

"That crazy woman is drying her wash with smoke," said the neighbors.

My mother really did hang her washing out any old how. She paid no attention to the season. She didn't bring things in when it rained. Sometimes she left them to the mercy of nighttime prowlers. Even if the line was free, she would often lay them out on the dew-drenched grass. But what the neighbors did not know was that my mother was not just hanging out her wash but making signals: the sheets spread out on the grass, anchored by stones, meant that the coast was clear and it was safe to come down from the mountain. If she left a single pair of pants on the line, you had to be careful because police were stationed where the two valleys met. When my mother hung only dresses on the line she was announcing the delivery of bundles of clandestine newspapers. A sole sheet on the clothes line along with a red skirt signified the arrival of weapons or a dangerous package. A bedspread meant that we could put someone up overnight. Only my mother was allowed to say that the way was clear and that the men of the sun could therefore come down into the valley. My mother did not speak: she sewed. That was her job. She had a mouth full of needles.

"Mama, I've put the fire out at the far end of the field."

"So go now and take the sheets down but leave the pants."

I knew a few of the codes. My father's shirt meant "Go round behind the graveyard"; my sister's skirt, "Beware – suspicious person!"; a pair of pants with one leg folded back, "Meeting the day after tomorrow as agreed."

My mother had taught me the secret language of drying the laundry. She was a virtuoso when it came to interrogative vowels, secret imperatives, and conjugations of shoelaces. Grammars of silence, unities of space rather than time, new coordinating conjunctions, agreements of past participles with auxiliary verbs that were neither the verb *être* nor the verb *avoir* – none of these held any mystery for her, for she was herself the mystery. But this morning, as I was eating my lunch, she suddenly rushed over to me and whispered: "Quick! Take your shirt off and go and hang it on the line, then bring back all the wash still there. Quick! Hurry up!"

I understood her haste when, from our garden which overlooked the road, I saw a long convoy of the gendarmerie's blue vans.

So my shirt was now part of a compound sentence. A letter at least, possibly a whole word. I was proud. I had been conjugated – I was almost a verb in my own right. I existed in my mother's secret language, an important word she had never used before, for it was the first time she wanted to leave my shirt all alone on the line.

So it was that I too, with my shirt, was speaking to the mountain. That shirt was a signal, a warning to "those on the other side." I ran towards the clothes line bare-chested. The vans on the road, just behind the barn, were disgorging dozens of security police armed with machine-guns. Their chief called to me just after I had hung up my shirt and was gathering up the sheets lying flat on the grass.

"Where do you live?"

I replied by pointing to the house behind me. He asked if I had seen any men coming down from the mountain. I told him no, then went back inside, noticing police hiding behind and all along the cemetery wall. No sooner was I through the door than my mother quickly relieved me of the sheets, which were not yet quite dry, and began ironing them methodically on the table. A sort of peace filled her eyes and she began to sing. That day I found out how to read in a way far beyond books. My shirt, all alone, fluttered like a poor man's flag. I was a semaphore unto myself. Nobody came down from the mountain and the security police down in their vans down on the road had left in their vans. Their "friends" on the other side must have misinformed them.

My mother has never abandoned the habits of her underground

days. Even today, every morning, she drapes washed clothes to dry all over the place. No one says she is crazy, because no one sees her. She spreads her things out inside the house, over chairs and in the most unlikely places. Every morning she remembers the days when freedom was built not with the mouth but with the hands.

My mother is still "building" freedom; she has preserved its signs. Her underclothes scattered about the shack are still unknown letters intended to be read by heaven through the window. The washing is always hung up, in the single room where she lives, because one must always be on the lookout for ways to help the belly of freedom give birth at short notice to a new child.

In her shack she is forever expecting a *compañero* from the other side to come down into the valley with his heavy pack, exhausted. Her words are still pants, bed sheets, torn pullovers, black dresses like flags, underwear, dungarees, and tattered bedspreads. These days the mountains are inside her shack, and so is her freedom.

It seems to me that even here she is helping those "from the other side" to get through, for even though they are nowhere to be seen, and even if there is no more "other side," the security police are still everywhere and their presence needs to be signaled.

I no longer want the doctor to come and see her. My mother's mind is all there. It is the doctor who does not understand. The Civil War is not yet over.

—

La Cega

THEY CALLED HER La Cega. In the language of beyond the mountains, *cega* meant blind. La Cega was either Grandma or the Old Woman – it depended who was talking. The boy did not know her real name because she had always been called La Cega. Each morning she touched his face and traced his features with her fingers. He loved this hand stroking his head. In the house with her chair and her cane she waited for the sun, begging for its light as she groped her way along the wall. From her corner by the hearth to the window, from the door to the bed, then back to the window. Her cane was the hand of a secret clock whose time only the boy could tell. All day long she followed the movements of sun and shadows. It was as if she were directing the light with her stick.

We all knew what time of day it was from La Cega's location. When she was sitting down, not far from the flowers and near the dishes, it was getting on for nine o'clock. When she was at the second window it was ten – time for the mailman to come in and wish her good morning. When La Cega went to the hallway, where the front door was open summer and winter, it was noon. At four in the afternoon she would be by the back door. And when night fell time-telling was over, and she would tend the fire. La Cega was a flesh-and-blood clock keeping time in our valley.

"What time is it?"

"Look for La Cega and you'll find out," my father used to say.

La Cega was over a hundred years old. She had outlived short breath, failed dreams, dead fires, and lost eyes. Her saliva produced apparitions of birds, dogs of dust, and men with fistfuls of knives. A face known to her alone drew near every night, making the stars shine more brightly. The old woman kissed that face come from within her hollow eyes for a long time. She washed it with silence. She attached a past to it that was wrenched from a future itself arisen from the past.

Her cane and her straw-bottomed chair were the regalia of her royal standing as widow of the light. With her white eyes La Cega saw everything, in front of her and behind her, inside and outside and above and below her grotto of light. People feared her because she saw what they could not see. La Cega treated the boy as her eyes. She kissed him too from within her own eyes. La Cega used to call the stars the night's eyes and flowers the day's.

The boy often asked La Cega to sing. Standing before the open window, she would seem then to be looking at herself in a mirror. She was the light, the light that came in through the window. La Cega was the window looking at the light. La Cega brought the day in behind the light.

At first she would not want to sit down. She would bat away a fly that only she could see. A kind of prayer. She would add a piece of wood to the fire and push smoldering logs around with her cane. It was her job to call up memories and poke the fire. Only after a while, once a flame began to lick at the wood, did she start gently stroking the boy's head.

"Cega, sing to me in your language."

And she always made the same reply: "But why do you want me to sing in a language that nobody speaks and that is good only for dogs?"

And then in her scratchy voice, like a little girl with gray hair, rocking back and forth, La Cega would begin to mumble verses in a language that neither day, nor schoolteachers, nor books, nor night could understand.

The sky was dull. Amidst the thorn bushes the men were drying themselves with the torn rags of their lost republic. The language of the North had traveled upriver, following paths that moons ate up along with iron insects. Hope was a locked book of water opened from time to time by a lightning bolt. La Cega's language was as secret as a key, an egg, a knife.

It was the language of the hill that sloped down to the first church, of the field with the three fig trees, of the horizontal gaps in the sky, and of the ropes that escaped the boy's grasp as he hauled trees from the meadow toward the river. A language that traveled on down to the plain, barking and chasing after the horses. It followed the valley as far as the boulder that furnished the old time to the entire bottomland. It was said that the devil had passed that way once, gliding above a wild stream, and when nearby goats failed to recognize him he turned them into rocks for evermore. But, as the old woman confided to the boy one day, there were certain nights when, warmed by the moon, those rocks came back to life and began to move about.

Along with La Cega the boy understood the secret of the cloud and the eagle's shadow as well as the law of the smoke around the sun. He learned about the silence of the stunted flower by the church, about the quavering logics of dust, and about butterflies lashed by the salty spittle of horses.

La Cega stuffed herself with sand. She chewed the wind and pieces of broken birds. In her mouth was a house built then blasted by a storm. A house that she bought and sold incessantly as she went in and out the door. At the top of the stairs in this house was a window beyond which the sky passed and never turned back. La Cega was the instant that halted the progression of the day. In her mouth too was an eye observing everything that spoke.

La Cega would sing. The boy told himself that Saint Francis, whose statue kept watch over the crossroads, must also speak her language, because the animals understood him. Each time the two went for a walk, La Cega, pointing to the statue covered in bird lime, would say: "Look, the birds love him. They could go and shit somewhere else, but they only shit on him!"

The boy's father, a road worker, also had something in common with animals. He too had a private language that only certain people understood. Those building the road along the river were all foreigners: some from beyond the mountains at the head of the second valley and some who had come back from the two concentration camps by the sea. The father had crossed the mountains to get to the plateau in the depths of winter before his son was born.

One day at noon, after getting out of school, the boy had raced yelling towards the new road and the heaps of steaming tar that he took for caramel. The stuff had a Sunday smell to it, but the unknown confectioners shoveling this delight across the roadway shouted to him not to come any closer or he would get burnt.

The language understood the stars. It answered the clouds. It was an ugly language, thick with bone and gravel. A language that gathered spit and forced it between the teeth, then came back by way of the nose and ended up at the back of the throat with a rasping tree-like sound. It sounded like bulls. Or like horses. Dog language spat cock's crowing amid the *h*'s and *m*'s that vowels separated like green-wood pickets immune to fire itself.

Everyone was afraid of La Cega because she spoke dog language. Never did she speak to a dog in French but always in its own tongue. Whenever she sang secretly to the boy in that language, dogs would come and lie whining at her feet as if they understood her.

La Cega would say: "Watches injure time."

La Cega had two gold watches that did not work and that she wore simultaneously, one on each wrist. When she wanted to leave she would say *"Es tiempo."* It is time.

La Cega knew time. On her watch leaking water had washed off the numbers and the hands had been stilled by eyes looking at them too much. Dozens of times and weeks of figures had crowded into the watch's circle of signs.

She would say: "Gold stops time."

The hours of her watch were wooden boards fixed to crucified little lights and tiny ravines. She had a jewel box containing piles of watches that didn't work. She knew it was time that dwelt there, buried amidst the rings and bracelets.

She would say: "A watch needs to be wrong."

When a watch doesn't work it is because it is consulting another watch. Watches ask one another for the time, and some watches prefer to die so as to be still closer to the great time that circles above us. Every watch restarts the series of all watches.

La Cega would say: "A real watch never tells the time."

Stopped watches weave invisible garments for numbers. With their fragile hands they fashion circles that they slip around the wrists of the dead.

———

Dog Language

THE DOG WAITED patiently for the boy to regurgitate the meat. But the boy ingested the morsel whole, for, to avoid vomiting, he had thrown his head back. With the open newspaper lying in the mud, he tore the meat apart. It was a piece from the belly, the butcher had said. Bloody, some of it almost black with iron, lumps of it went down his throat and filled it with their barbarity. The bluish parts, streaked with white and yellow tendons, turned pink as the boy tore at them. The bitter taste, at times almost sweet, overwhelmed his nostrils and taste buds and made him want to throw up at every mouthful. This was the first time he had eaten raw meat. He gulped down everything without chewing as though in a hurry to finish, repressing a retch from time to time. The dog at his feet, usually calm and obedient, gazed at him hungrily, its eyes full of frustration.

The dog had devoured everything it could. Now it was eyeing a richly marbled piece dangling from the boy's lips because he couldn't swallow it. The red, half-chewed hunk hung from the delicately sculpted human mouth like a bloody hand with its fingers cut off. The dog thought that the boy was sticking his tongue out. Then the boy jerked the morsel from his mouth and gave it to the dog.

The boy watched the dog swallow the meat and, unable to help it, started throwing up over the animal's head. This further excited the dog's mad hunger for flesh. Its gaze no longer fixed on the boy's mouth, it began wolfing down the pieces that had been spewed up and now lay around it. The boy had regurgitated everything, but he had to keep on eating the meat. So he picked a piece up again and began chewing it with eyes shut.

The idea of eating raw meat had first come to him when, with his mother in the butcher's shop, he saw a whiteboard on which, in shimmering red letters, he read:

MEAT FOR DOGS!

The boy immediately thought of La Cega, who spoke to him in dog language and he decided that this meat was reserved for him and La Cega. His mother, however, took him by the arm and whispered in his ear so that the butcher would not hear: "We mustn't buy any of that meat. If we eat it, it might kill us."

The boy concluded that the language of La Cega could kill, and that there must be a special meat for words and for knowledge of the deep secrets behind speech. Might La Cega have gone blind because of eating "meat for dogs"?

The boy waited for the butcher's van. He had spent three days longing to buy meat for dogs. He chose the moment when the butcher was packing up to ask the man for dog meat. The man tossed him some horsemeat wrapped in newspaper, telling him that the dogs would have a feast and assuring him that the meat was fresh.

Trembling, the boy thrust the package under his shirt. He went round the back of the house to find the dog, which was in its kennel. In the ditch by the fig tree he opened up the blood-soaked newspaper. And then, without any consultation between boy and dog, the two fell upon the meat.

Even though he was afraid of dying or of going blind like La Cega, the boy swallowed the raw, bloody pieces of horsemeat one after another. He was sure of it: he too was going to speak La Cega's language – but then, would he not lose his own language and start barking like a dog? The idea flashed through his mind, but he remembered that La Cega spoke two languages but did not bark like a dog.

The boy got to his feet and set off at a run down the road. New words began to bark in his throat. The dog's red eyes fastened on his mouth in hopes of another attack of nausea. But the boy deliberately forced himself not to vomit again. He must become a dog if he was going to speak the language of La Cega. Once back at the house he could not help retching when the dog barked.

Like a clock on two legs, dressed all in black, La Cega was waiting for him at the door. She was mumbling verses in a tongue that only angels and ghosts understand. She gave the boy her hand. As they walked along, they deliberately overturned ashcans of stars. The boy knew that it was night now and that time was no more. Clinging to the dress of the old woman so as not to fall, he began to sing in dog language.

Cherry Thief

THE BIRDS HAVE stopped checking the shadows. The light flows through the leaves in a black stream. Behind me a bee is drinking up time. My hands grasp the highest stone in the wall and then, silently, I hoist myself over onto the cherry tree. Stealing a cherry is a rite of freedom. The child and the thief belong to the same family. Eating a cherry is stealing it. Looking at a cloud is likewise a way of removing it. Icarus forgot to steal the air before growing wings on his back. Falls always have a cause.

The memory of the first theft is always the memory of the original crisis, a feeling of sin like an explosion in your mouth. All the same, the cherry stolen from a garden cherry tree by scaling a forbidden wall on a June evening has the taste of happiness.

All children are cherry thieves. Even today I cannot imagine buying cherries from a market stall, and I always catch myself grabbing a handful and slipping them quickly into my bag. You don't buy cherries, you steal them while awaiting the fulminations of an old man all riled up and racing down the garden row, gun in hand.

Every June, in the bird-thronged tree behind the church, fat black cherries awaited us. We were like armed sparrows: we did not ask permission and we were ever willing to scatter in every direction on a quest for fresh thievery. We had a special technique for eating our cherries: we did not breathe, and we stored the stones in our cheeks, in reserve for the bombardiering that would follow the feast. We organized contests with mouths full of stones, but they were mute contests, oddly silent, like flights of birds in the sky, so that the tree's elderly owner would not hear us. And then, as per our custom, each standing on a branch, we would piss on the hives on the other side of the wall and take off as fast as our legs could carry us down the lane before the bees could exercise their legitimate right to vengeance.

One morning, however, for an hour now, I had not been stealing but simply eating the cherries of *Tiet* Gibraltar – my "uncle from the sea." Mama had sent me to him to get vine shoots for a snail bake. My uncle lived in a refuse dump behind the co-operative. His house was surrounded by a fence made of old planks and tires held together with wire. A well at the bottom of his garden supplied a sandy and salty water that we took care to filter before we drank it.

Uncle Gibraltar was short and dark. His crabbed fingers, like licorice sticks, were forever stroking a dog lying between his feet. I always saw him digging in his garden. Uncle Gibraltar was from far away, as his name seemed to suggest. He was not my aunt's husband, though the pair had been shacked up since the Civil War. So he was just a courtesy uncle to me, but you were never to say that he was not married to my aunt.

In his garden my uncle had planted twelve fruit trees in a circle, like the hours on a clock face, and to a keen observer their shadows were hands that really told the time. In the center was a majestic spreading fig tree under which my uncle would sit shaded from the sun from spring to fall. Enthroned there on seats from an old stripped car, he watched his own shadow turn and lengthen toward his memories until it turned them around so they seemed to come from the future. Never did I steal fruit from my uncle. You could steal only beyond the bounds of the family – a circle roughly three kilometers in diameter, as my father counseled me. Once outside that circle everything was permitted; allowed; within it, nothing was. Such was the law that ensured our peace.

Uncle Gibraltar saw me coming from far away. When I was close, a few steps from his shadow, I greeted him with the words "Mama sent me for some bines for the snails."

He did not answer me, but pointed to the cherry tree as an invitation to pick the fruit. I had two bags with me and had been counting on taking a few cherries home. Naturally I stuffed myself like a pig, taking care not to swallow a bee for which I had become a seriously devoted competitor. I felt Uncle Gibraltar's presence somewhere behind me. He was proud that I was eating his cherries. Then he suddenly came up to the foot of the tree and said, "You don't even know what you are eating."

Of course I replied that on the contrary I did know, that I was eating cherries.

"No. You are not eating cherries. It is Guillermo Ganuza that you are eating. This tree, this cherry tree, is called Guillermo Ganuza. You are eating Guillermo Ganuza."

I did not understand. I wondered why my uncle gave men's names to trees, though I knew some people in the village who gave people's names to dogs. True, I had noticed long ago that certain trees bore little signs at their feet, carefully branded with mysterious names. But I had assumed, since my uncle was a keen amateur botanist, that these were either the Latin names of the various species or the names of weed-killers, and I had never bothered to read them.

"This tree is named Guillermo Ganuza Navarro. You never read its sign? You have been eating from it for years but you don't know its name? Every tree here is a man."

I deciphered my uncle's writing and, pronouncing each syllable separately, read out the sign at the foot of the cherry tree: "Guillermo Ganuza Navarro."

Intrigued now, I walked all around the orchard. Under the peach tree, the sign read simply Josep Sabaté Llopart. The apple tree bore the name of Antonio Franquesa Fumoll. The pear tree was Simon Gracia Fleringan, and the plum Josep López Penedo. At the foot of the lemon tree was a bicycle wheel, and on each spoke a letter on a piece of cardboard: painstaking small capitals spelt out the name F.R.A.N.C.I.S.C.O. S.A.B.A.T.É. Engraved on a birdhouse hanging from the orange tree, in florid lettering, were the words Francisco Denís Diez. In the apricot tree was a smiling photograph of Martín Ruiz Montoya, with a special mention of "Barcelona." Directly into the bark of the olive tree my uncle had carved Ramón Vila Capdevila (Caraquemada), and, in big capitals, VIVA. On the banana tree bark had grown over the first letter of a first name: *ablo*. My uncle had planted a tree for each of his network comrades who had been assassinated between 1949 and 1960.

"And this one?" I asked, pointing to the hazel, which had no sign.

"That one? That one is me. You will inscribe my name on it when I am gone."

We were not supposed to pronounce my uncle's real name. It was a secret. Because of the police, my father said. To this day I never say it. You never know.

Amongst ourselves we always called him either *Tiet del Mar* or Uncle Gibraltar. He made jam with the fruit from his trees and gave it away, as winter came on, out of "solidarity" and for the children of the political prisoners. You never saw him after that until spring, when his trees were blossoming. He was happy when I ate his cherries.

For a long time this was all I remembered of him. And then, later, other moments came back to me that seemed to emerge from the future. It was perhaps then that the fantastical notion occurred to me of writing words on tree branches. This morning I am thinking of a tree and the tree's offspring. Of the tree's milk. Of the tree's mother. I review all the trees that have lost their human names in the forest.

Now I see my uncle again, Uncle Gibraltar, his arms full of apples that are not apples but men's heads. Now that bloody laundry is bubbling in a flag-draped washtub. Now that there are no more trees. Now that the dead hold onto our legs to keep us standing up. Now that I am motionless, contemplating little pasts that I sometimes take for the present. Now that there are no more flags.

Meticulously, letter by letter, I carve "Tiet del Mar" on the hazel tree. Not his real name. You never know. As I watch the sap run, I plunge into its eyes, spitting out cherry pits. Like memories, or bullets from a pistol.

As our family friend Margherita still often says, when she goes into the garden, "Our pistols are old but our bullets make new holes."

The Scarab's Revenge

SANTAMARÍA TOOK ME by the hand and gave me more advice on how best to approach the man I wanted to kill: "Don't forget, you should never focus on the center but always just away from the center, and that goes for a star, a rat, or for that matter a fly. If you want to hit a bird in full flight, don't fire when you have it in your sights but aim ahead of it, so that your bullet goes to the place where the bird in motion will encounter it. If you aim at your target itself, the bird will escape the bullet by outpacing it and the projectile will go to waste in its wake."

Then Santamaría opened a jar full of scorpions, picking one of them up and carefully placing it in an empty matchbox.

"At the last moment," he went on, "take your live scorpion and slip it into a glass of hard liquor. You will see it struggling. Be sure to remember before you drink which way the scorpion turns first. That is the angle from which you will attack and deliver your first thrust."

"Should I swallow the scorpion live?" I asked him, looking sideways at the killer he had chosen for me, which was trying to rear up in its box.

"When you see that the Little Creature is no longer moving, and that it has drowned, you can drink the rum. But do not swallow the Little Creature as though you were trying to bring back a lost love. Along with the rum all its spirit of hatred will enter into you and inhabit you from now on. Keep the dead Little Creature under your tongue. Before opening your knife, push it out between your lips and spit it at the feet of your enemy. In his eyes you will see the dawn of a tortured fear of the scorpion."

Throwing a fly into a small fire he had just started with straw in a black clay pot, Santamaría concluded with these words: "Oh Lord of the Three Powers, preserve us from the vengeance of the earth and of the venom eater!"

At first light on this day, live scorpions had to be collected for certain secret and higher deadly purposes. Ever so cautiously, Santamaría would capture Little Creatures by describing a circle around them with his stick, then coaxing them one by one into a leather pouch which he later emptied into a metal box. For the scorpion kills like a contortionist, its flanks folded over an invisible rod and a fiery dagger held between its ankles of iron.

"Oh Lord of the Three Powers, preserve us from the vengeance of the earth and of the venom eater!"

A Little Creature was scuttling through the dust.

As was his custom, Santamaría placed his foot gently on the killer's head and watched the vain thrashing of its lethal tail. With his knife he cut off the tail, picked it up delicately and placed it in the leather bag hanging at his waist. Then he continued on his way, following the zigzag tracks of other scorpions.

"When a Little Creature crawls under your left foot," he said, "it should be cut in two and its tail saved for death. When one crawls under your right foot, you save its head for love. If it crawls in front of you, you keep it for courage." Then, once again, between clenched teeth: "Oh Lord of the Three Powers, preserve us from the vengeance of the earth and of the venom eater!"

Santamaría went down to the riverbed along a pathway of stones and trees whitened like the vertebrae of a great stretched-out skeleton. The sun dazzled him briefly and he cast a furtive glance to his left. Another Little Creature had halted on the rocks. Yet again he intoned: "Oh Lord of the Three Powers, preserve us from the vengeance of the earth and of the venom eater!" And with lightning speed he scooped the Little Creature up into his leather pouch, which he then emptied with a flick of the wrist into the metal box.

Over the morning Santamaría caught nineteen black scorpions and just one that was all white – almost transparent. "This Little Creature is the most powerful," he said. "You take no more than seven breaths after it stings you. Little Creatures are like stars. Never look a distant star right in the eye, or you will not see it. You must look just alongside it. Only when you proceed in this way can you see it, the very center of it."

Santamaría kicked a tree stump with his bare foot, causing dozens – a veritable hailstorm – of scorpions to pour out onto the ground.

"If stars are the eyes of the night, Little Creatures are the eyes of the desert. You must look at them sideways also, if you want to see and understand them."

Santamaría sold scorpions, spiders and snakes, dried badgers, remains of birds, and braided amulets made from horses' tails or women's hair. At the town market everyone was familiar with the power of his homemade cures for stomach ailments, alienated affections and jealousy, backaches, headaches, dysentery, and every kind of fatal malady.

Santamaría was the finest teller of souls and reverser of fortunes for miles and miles around. Nine days after the death of a child people would come to consult him and, standing by a crate with a red candle burning on it, he would speak in the voice of the deceased. But what made the Master stand out from all the other healers who swarmed in the valley was his scorpion tea.

"Drink it down all at once," he would say, "and you'll see your vigor return and tackle whatever confronts you."

—

Santamaría revitalized old men and fertilized childless young couples and helped women retrieve the love of men who had left them for someone younger. Mixed with an old corn spirit that burnt your stomach like flaming gasoline, his tea built up the strength and ensured the success of anyone out for vengeance for an infidelity or dishonor. Santamaría could see in the night and interpret images in the sun without looking away.

As I was wrapping the matchbox containing the live scorpion in my handkerchief, I observed Santamaría's face. His eyes were separated by a long scar running down the middle of his forehead, testament to a blow from a machete that he had managed to deflect one night during a brawl with a hunter. Ever since, Santamaría's face had resembled a hand. He did not look at things: rather, he stole them with his eyes. His nose was a finger that breathed and his mouth was a thumb and forefinger that he clamped together when he spoke. His ears were yet other hands that grabbed words floating in the air.

Santamaría did not look at the living: rather, he stripped them down to their dead bodies. When you spoke to Santamaría you had to look at him sideways – the way you look at the stars.

Looking sidelong was a mark of courtesy. When words were spoken, the gaze had to conform to a ritual geometry that contained and guided them. By describing triangles and hypotenuses with his hands and semicircles with his feet, Santamaría prevented the listener from saying certain things.

Looking someone straight in the eye signaled death. Thus when I conversed with Santamaría I was always hovering between life and death. During each conversation there was a moment when you had to look down at the ground so as to be neutral, and you were always obliged to strike a balance between those words that could be uttered while looking right in the eye and those which were to be delivered obliquely. Knowing how to speak meant knowing how to observe what you were saying.

"The eyes we have are only minor eyes, for our real eyes are on our backs. If the Little Creature looks at you with its tail it is because it kills you with its tail. Dying means closing the eyes on your back."

Santamaría had learnt in the forest how to create living brooches with scarabs, whose carapace he scored lightly so as to insert chips of amethyst and blue shell. He would then attach the insect's body to a piece of wood with a tiny chain.

On returning home, fashionable city ladies would carefully remove their living brooch, which they had been sporting at their shoulder, and place it gingerly in a pot by a potato or avocado plant on which it would feed avidly.

In the village all the women went about with their living jewel on its chain, while the men avoided looking at it for fear of bewitchment or amorous enslavement.

It is said that one day Santamaría had set an emerald and diamond chips in the wings of a scarab for a foreigner who paid him with a thick wad of dollar bills. He had then meticulously cut out the green eye of God featured on each of these notes and stuck them at eye level on the wooden walls of his shack. The remainder of the bills he had reduced to ashes in a ceremony that incorporated photographs of lottery winners clipped from an old newspaper and displayed between images of an iguana and an owl.

These eyes of God protected the center of his house and paralyzed with respect all who entered it in search of his counsel. His medicine was indisputably the strongest for bringing good luck, and people came to his house one after another for a prayer to the Virgin under the staring, timeless, and reduplicated eyes from the dollar bills.

As a general rule, however, Santamaría did not inlay scarab wings with precious stones; rather, he bought sour candy drops from the market, bit off chips and stuck these onto the insects.

"The spirit of the scarab loves women because it carries every color. A color is an eye that watches the color that resides in time and within things. Women are the true guardians of color: they prevent colors from taking their revenge in a single night by becoming all the nights that black out the day."

One morning the Mayor, Don Isidro Zapato, the largest landowner in the area, son of Don Isidro Joan Zapato, leader of the province's Catholic Party and husband of a conquistador's descendant, decided he wanted to give a present to his favorite daughter, Doña Inés. Having heard tell of the magic powers of the Master's living jewels, he thought that such a scarab would protect her from misfortune.

Don Isidro Zapato was an oily individual whose reputation for cruelty surpassed anything known in the valley or even in the mountains. *Sotto voce*, people called him *Zapo*, or Toad, and a favorite game of the village children was to roast a wretched batrachian until it exploded as a riposte to his proclamations and diktats. "Doing a toad" developed into a sport practiced almost daily outside police stations and other seats of authority. Practical jokers regularly opened up sacks of toads in front of Don Isidro's mansion or threw them over the wall into the banks of roses and flowerbeds of the Japanese garden that was his pride and joy.

Don Isidro Zapato, the largest landowner in the area, son of Don Isidro Joan Zapato, leader of the province's Catholic party, and husband of a conquistador's descendant, knew that they called him Toad. Whenever he heard a croaking, his brow blanched and he began to perspire over his blank notebooks and his speeches. The rainy season became an absolute nightmare for his bodyguards, who were ordered to hunt down the humiliating batrachians day and night. He even issued an edict banning the release of toads in the town and regulating their sale and transport under the pretext that they were a species under threat of extinction and in need of protection; any infringement courted imprisonment.

But there was nothing for it. At official events a perfect imitation of the call of the toad from an unknown source invariably reached the assembly hall, a croaking that sullied the glass chandeliers and the white shirts of the guests. "Toad to the swamp! Toad to the swamp! A lighted cigarette to blow up Toad!" The cries of the people battered walls and blew in windows before fading away in the mansion's remotest grounds. One year, on the first day of Carnival, a new mask made its appearance in the midst of the crowd: that of a toad, destined, naturally, to be raised high and burnt in front of the governor's mansion. Don Isidro Zapato, the largest landowner in the area, son of Don Isidro Joan Zapato, leader of the province's Catholic party, and husband of a conquistador's descendant, never did win the Battle of the Toad.

Santamaría knew Toad. In the days of the land occupations, by all accounts, his mother had perished when her house was set on fire by soldiers.

"If you don't tell us where your husband is hiding," the soldiers' commander had said, "you will burn with your shack."

The mother had said nothing, and the house had burned down, with her in it, like a lake of bubbling rocks. On the same day her brother went mad after soldiers had forced Coca-Cola under pressure up his nose to make him talk. Thereafter, in the village, he wandered around humming and shrieking whenever he saw a fire.

Santamaría called his revenge The Thing.

The Thing went round and round in his head like a wild compass needle. North was anywhere. Sometimes The Thing grabbed hold of him like a lady of the night and plunged him into alcohol and the mirrors that you cannot see. Often it left him asleep on the floor with his dogs, under his hammock, until noon. But one spring morning The Thing in flesh and blood came to pay him a visit in the shape of an envoy from the mayor who knocked on his door wishing to place an order for a living brooch.

Who would ever have recognized in this man – in this brewer of herbal teas – that ten-year-old boy, the head of whose decapitated horse had once been thrown into the pool of the spring on the family farm?

Anyway, The Thing itself came knocking at Santamaría's door in the shape of the emissary of the very one whom The Thing was supposed to strike. And so it was that the day after the visit from the Mayor's messenger, Santamaría conceived the idea of combining a scorpion and a scarab for the living brooch of Toad's daughter Doña Inés.

Santamaría knew scarabs, and he knew scorpions. But how could he conceal a scorpion in a scarab? The feat was daunting, not to say impossible. A scarab could not be opened up and a live scorpion placed in its belly. Nor could a scorpion be slipped beneath a precious stone or disguised by an artificial color.

Santamaría gave much thought to The Thing over several nights and reached the conclusion that the answer lay in the small piece of wood he used to moor the chain holding the scarab captive to its carapace. He considered the fact that every evening a scarab needed to be placed not in a jewel box but rather on a plant upon which it fed, near the dressing-table, with its chain fast to the piece of wood. This piece of wood, the mobile base of the jewel, was meant to be pinned as a brooch to a dress or blouse.

For three days and three nights Santamaría worked patiently on the piece of wood, no bigger than a thumbnail, that anchored the little chain. Meticulously, he dug into the wood, smoothing the sides of the aperture with his knife, as if designing a miniature coffin or crib. This done, he used a pair of tweezers to insert a tiny reddish scorpion, one of those whose sting can precipitate a drawn-out, fevered, and ineluctable death. Last, using a little corn-flour paste, he sealed the cavity with a wood chip, just next to the fastener for the little chain.

Santamaría used his stick to trace a sign in the earth which he immediately erased with a bare foot.

"This is how The Thing will be consummated. I know that Doña Inés wants to wear the brooch at the Mass of San Fermín, and that, as is the town custom, it is her father who will attach the piece of wood to the collar of her blouse. At the slightest pressure the seal will break, the Little Creature will escape and Toad will be stung."

"But Master, how can you tell that the scorpion will not sting Doña Inés but pick her father instead?"

"Remember what I told you: if you want to catch a Little Creature, look to the side of it, just as you would if you wanted to focus on a star. The same applies in the case of your enemy. Death is also a star in the night. You must not look it straight in the face, or it will split in two and come at you from behind and kill you."

After sealing the fragile cover, Santamaría chose a scarab with brilliant green wings to which he affixed two emerald chips. As a finishing touch he laid a blue canary feather on the insect's head.

"Oh Lord of the Three Powers, preserve us from the vengeance of the earth and of the eater of the three venoms!"

Everything turned out just as Santamaría had foreseen. Before the Mass, just as Toad was detaching the scarab from its wooden support in order to pin the latter to his daughter's blouse, the wood split open and the red scorpion emerged from its hiding-place and stung him between his fingers. Toad tried to cry out, but his tongue was immediately paralyzed. A dull pain surged through his arm and white foam dribbled from his mouth.

No one, except for Toad, had seen the scorpion surface from within the piece of wood that held the scarab by a little gold chain. Not even Doña Inés, though she was standing before her father as she waited for her gift. True, a few policemen said that a scorpion had fallen out of the tree under which the mayor had been standing. But in that dry season, when trees and plants must draw nourishment from deep under the earth, nobody saw any connection between Santamaría and the scorpion.

"Vengeance is an art as difficult as the art of love. It is not given to everyone to take revenge," Santamaría would say. "Vengeance is the highest form of forgiveness. When you take revenge on earth, you do not take it in heaven, and a person who dies like a child in the arms of vengeance wins eternal salvation. Getting revenge avoids a Mass."

Santamaría had slept with his vengeance after the fashion of a madly jealous lover. Every night he had slowly undressed it and hung it on the posts of his bedstead. Then he would begin to caress it with the tips of his fingernails, tattooing its skin with white and obscure tracks. But only death could satisfy the Master's dark companion. He would leave it alive until dawn, causing it to cry out in fury and despair. Then he would free it, but keep its arms shackled so that it could not obtain gratification on its own without its night-time counterpart.

Santamaría had concentrated all the love in the world until the world's end on his vengeance. Santamaría loved vengeance. Vengeance loved him and caused shrubs to flower in front of his shack. That night, after the death of Toad, Santamaría untied the hands of The Thing and, pushing it back down onto the floor, a dark lover, possessed it with great thrusts of his loins to the point of death. The Thing had the body of a dancer and created rivulets of sweat on the earth, while its rattling groans pierced the night as far as the drunken women still sleeping in the streets. As the Master's wife for eternity, The Thing always made love with a knife rusted by the moon. The two of them, drenched in sweat, engaged in a tit-for-tat of deep wounds and shrieks. And then, with a last pelvic shove and a long cruel close-lipped kiss, Santamaría killed The Thing, like an invisible woman, at the very moment of Toad's death.

The thing was done and The Thing would no longer come to visit him. The Thing was stronger than its name, vengeance. It was almost daybreak and the donkeys were already hee-hawing on the farms when Santamaría in his sleep dragged the invisible body of The Thing down to the river and threw it in. The dark dancer floated for a few moments among the logs coming down from the mountain, then vanished in the torrent rushing beneath the rocks on its way to the sea.

Santamaría woke at noon, all alone for the first time in his life, in the cords of his hammock swinging between the two posts of its stand. That day the moon passed in front of the sun and all of a sudden the birds fell silent.

Toad's death was celebrated with all the pomp and all the accolades that befitted his rank. The corpse was embalmed, shaven, and perfumed. The bishop delivered the funeral oration in person. The luminaries of the administration were on hand. Likewise the prefect of police, all the big landowners, and all the main members of the Party. During the service, however, a whole cortege of toads made itself heard in the church tower, in the street, and even behind the altar during the elevation. When, at the cemetery, a toad from the mud of the last rainfall leapt onto the casket, everyone took this as a sign of fate.

It is well known that, at death, a life's lines come together as a double that leaves our body. This double disappears into the eyes of other, live people whom we do not see, but who wander through our dreams.

"Toad is dead! Toad is dead!"

The cry reverberated through hovels, prisons, and cooking pots. Among the village populace fires were lit. But the celebration was gentle, muted, without singing, and lamps and cigars were shielded for fear that soldiers on patrol might fire on the red flares that signaled people smoking. Around five o'clock Santamaría went to the cemetery. On an anonymous headstone he placed another scarab, its wings inset with emerald and adorned with shards of candy drops and a canary feather. He tidied up the grave, placing rice and meatballs alongside flowers. He also dug a little gutter leading from the grave to the ditch, because the rains would be coming.

"By tomorrow the soul of a woman will have eaten everything by way of the stars," he said. "The clouds and rain foretold by the bad moon are on the way."

"The Thing is finished," Santamaría told me. "The Thing is happy. The Thing is sleeping now in the river. The Thing will never return."

Grabbing hold of a burning log, he uttered incomprehensible and irremediable words with his mouth closed, words that that no one could understand. Except, perhaps, for the dead – and those among the living who were still caressing a Thing with their fingernails as they waited for the right moment to kill.

"Our strength lies in knowing how to look to the side in order

—

to see the center of what we see. Each thing here below is a star, and we all have a shadow that follows us even at high noon. Only The Thing can redeem human beings. Only The Thing."

Santamaría thrust his hands into the fire, looking me straight in the face for the first time. After a moment I lowered my own gaze and noticed that the fire was popping the skin on his knuckles. It was as if his hands wanted to eat the flames or to separate them and braid them with the smoke like a woman's hair. During this painful purification not a murmur came from his mouth until he began to sing an unknown song in a deep voice as he struck the fire with the flat of his hands:

My betrothed cuts the cords
My betrothed loves not the earth
and is burning my house down

Suddenly the wind pushed the door open and the flickering candlelight made the green god's eyes on the walls, clipped from dollar bills, begin to dance. Santamaría went outside and scrutinized the stars in the night. From each one he drew down threads that he wove into a garment to protect us from the world. Was there someone way up there on a star, he wondered, who was gazing at the earth, where he was, and pulling on an endless thread?

Santamaría wondered whether, on the point of a needle, lost in the dark, there was not another man explaining to a young fiancé of death how to catch scorpions without dying. For on the far side of the infinite, Santamaría's double knew that he was there, looking at him. On the far side there was another him, and his mission on earth was to help the one who was on the far side, but who was at the same time him, complete the building of awareness that he had undertaken.

Dying meant reuniting with this other, this absolute brother who was looking at him, eating in unison with him in the mirror that separated the two of them. When both had finished their last meal and ripped up all the images of their lives, they would depart, each leaving his remains on one side of the infinite. Their freed souls would fly toward one another attracted by the magnet of a love that knew more than love. They would found a star with their reunited soul in a forge of the infinite. For Santamaría the day was an illusion just like the night, and it was the alliance between a day and a night that you cannot see which created the true fire of fire's immortality. Shadow and light divided the two faces of a being that are always reunited at death. Human beings on earth were merely the silent spectators of this reunion.

"It is going to rain light on the mountain," he said, pointing with a trembling finger into the obscurity. "The eagles are coming down to enter our dreams and take us into a slumber unknown to us that will awaken us for evermore."

—

Santamaría had studied the science of shadow and light. In his isolated shack, he had laid down the fundamental laws of the universe. For him the day was the shadow of the day and the night the shadow of the night. Each object belonged to a pair of twin objects whose perfect similarity could never be qualified. Thus the day was never the shadow of the night, nor the night ever the shadow of the day. The blending of shadow and light was the foundation of the supreme and secret wisdom of this doctor of the stars living in a shack.

I also sought to discern shadows in the hierarchy of clouds and to wrench new faces from the night. I heard a tree fall into the river.

Since the night before, soldiers had been marching along the far bank, their faces and bayonets painted black and their weapons sheathed in oilcloth for the river crossing.

Santamaría began to sing once more, then he went off with his bags of fabric and his staff covered with signs and bottle tops. He walked slowly, head back as he gazed at a group of stars coming down to him and pouring into his mouth, which thirst held open.

Santamaría drank the sky every night.

Suddenly I heard gunshots and the dull sound of a second tree falling into the river. When I turned around, I saw soldiers moving off and something ragged floating among the rocks and the logs.

It was Santamaría's jacket.

I ran along the riverbank trying to retrieve it, but the low arms of the trees tugged at my clothes and prevented me from getting close. I followed Santamaría's body, floodlit by the moon, as far as the rapids beyond the bridge. Then true night established its high and silent empire and I halted.

Santamaría knew that the shadows of the water dwelt in its crevices. He knew that the fish were souls of children, not yet born of women, whom the dead fished for from boats of bird feathers.

I was surprised to hear a voice not my own singing:

My betrothed loves not the earth
and drops flowers in the waters of the dead

The door of his shack was still open.

The Movies

WHEN WE WENT to the cinema, we left the house with chairs on top of our heads. Naturally we took the lousiest ones, the most caved-in, and the straw sticking out from the seats endowed us with hairy yellow wigs.

This was how, looking like African witch doctors, we covered the two kilometers that separated us from the picture show just beyond the border. Our faces, framed by the chairs' spindles, were hellish masks. We would hail one another from chair to chair: "Hello! Hello!"

Sometimes the chairs began to sing. These were odd processions, with no Virgin and no saints, headed to the beach despite the threat of mosquitoes or ghosts from the sea. We were monsters – or rather knights, Don Quijotes of the night in search of unlikely windmills. When it rained, the chairs were our umbrellas.

On the beach, the movie screen was set up next to the latrines. As for the stench, you couldn't tell whether it killed the mosquitoes or attracted them. There were different schools of thought, my father used to say.

Admission was not expensive, but we were the poorest of the

poor, so we would settle down behind a reed fence to see the film for free. We were the kings of the night.

When all went dark, we parted the reeds to watch the film. We were just behind the screen. For the sound, we were fine. Even too fine at times. At least we couldn't claim not to hear. On the other hand, the reverse subtitles put our eyes to the test.

Papa gave us peanuts and, if he had sold plenty of sardines that day, bought us popsicles from the ice cream man who was also just by the latrines.

We were little kings, Papa kept saying: when we had to pee we didn't have to go outside because we were already outside – and *already next to the toilets*. We didn't need to rile up the audience by pushing past people, and what was more the show was free.

We had no choice of picture. There were Charlie Chaplins, bottom-rung westerns, and a few Tarzans. Romantic films too, during which if a man and a woman kissed we had to shut our eyes or else Mama would give us a good whack.

Eventually we knew all the films by heart. We would tell people next to us what was going to happen next: "Cheeta is hiding up in the tree. Tarzan is going to screw a monkey. Jane has passed out. A croc is going to eat her." We exaggerated. We lied. We were taken for prophets.

The American films were subtitled. At first this ticked us off,

—

but we got used to it. Peering through the reeds, our whole family screwed up their eyes as they tried to decipher what could be read from the back side of the screen.

Papa would say "I couldn't care less. You can tell me about it later."

It was there, however, that we learned to read French – but back-to-front French, since we were behind the screen. My brother and I figured it out together, during the very same show:

"Me hungry."

"Where is Cheeta?"

"Up in the tree."

"Me love Jane."

"You lion my brother."

Little by little we learned to read all the subtitles with ease. We became experts. We would read them out loud for those who couldn't read them from either the front or the back. My brother even did sound effects. We were a real attraction and sometimes generated more interest than the film itself.

Before long, lots of people were joining us behind the reeds, less to see the picture than to hear us reading from behind the screen and doing sound effects. The public grew at every show – on our side of the screen.

The day came when we were more than a hundred behind the reed fence. This situation upset the projectionist, because he was losing a good many paying customers, and what was bound to happen happened: one evening he draped a green plastic tarp the full length of the fence. We could no longer either see or read anything. Unless, of course, we paid to go in at the entrance. This burned the whole family up, and by common accord we swore never to return.

My mother said we would be better off reading books. For a time we would read them backwards to remind us of the movies. Then we began to read them in the normal way. But now and again we would still read backwards, and it made us laugh.

Impressed by our virtuosity, Papa thought for a while that we might become politicians. My mother talked rather of the printing trade. My uncle, who made the rounds of the fairs with a caravan, thought he should take us on tour as a novelty act. In fact we were so gifted that Mémé, a grandmother by marriage, wanted to take us out of school since we were brighter than our teacher, who could only read forwards.

At school we stayed at the bottom of the class. We never did go back to the picture show.

—

The Piece of Wood

IT WAS AT first light that the grownups would get rid of the corpses by throwing them in the river.

But you had a chance to escape by hiding in one of the oil drums. After the evening soup I gathered leaves and slipped them under my blanket and placed stones on top to anchor things down and prevent the wind from revealing that I was gone. My head I replaced with the body of my dead dog. I had called him Dog because in that place nobody had a name.

I spread my scarf over Dog as though I were burying my own face. I felt that, from now on, the face I wore would be his. I kissed him and whistled gently into his ear as if I was calling him to come with me.

Goodbye dead Doggie. Goodbye dead Doggie.

Groping my way along the walls and scuttling from one hut to the next I taught myself to see with Dog's eyes, because I thought I was dead too. I was Dog's walking tomb, and I knew that on the other side of the world he was guarding the part of me that had died with him and would be waiting for me one day.

I melted into the shadows until I reached the monstrous line of trees swaying slowly like pendulums. I circled the dangling oil drums marked with a white cross – which was the grownups' way of indicating the ones containing dead bodies. Then, after lifting a lid, I slid into one of them alongside someone from Section 3 of the camp. His forehead was pressed against the metal side of the container as if he were asleep, but it was only his hands, clasped in a desperate prayer, that really gave the impression that he was alive.

I stayed next to him for several hours without looking at him. I fell asleep against his back. When I woke I thought it was Dog who had suddenly grown bigger since he had died and come back to me. But it was only the body of a dead boy that I as hugging.

The morning breeze had got up and the trees were creaking in the woods as their branches twisted this way and that. Gradually rain set up a relentless and regular tattoo on the oil drum. Its beat split my head in two. Then I heard footsteps on the gravel outside. It was the grownups come for the drums. I shifted the body of my dead companion and slid underneath him to avoid discovery. The grownups began to swear.

"Today there are a bunch of fucking rats in those barrels. With this rain we better make sure the truck doesn't get stuck in the mud."

I knew they called us rats when we were dead. I felt the grownups picking up my drum, placing it upright on the bed of their truck. I was afraid the lid might come off, but a grownup punched it firmly shut.

During the short journey to the river my companion's body moved and I wrapped my arms tightly around his belly. I was afraid that if ever his corpse slipped out of the drum they would spot me at the bottom.

"The river's going to burst its banks if this shit doesn't let up!" said one of the grownups who had stayed in the back to keep the drums upright.

The truck pulled up. I knew from the sound of the rapids that we had come to the end of the road. We were about to be tossed from the truck into the water. A perfect rat's funeral.

That night there were three oil drums.

Mine was the last.

The water flooded in straight away through the breathing holes and the drum rolled over. I had to use the boy's body for support as I popped the lid open. All of a sudden I was free of him and starting to swim for the far bank with the help of the current.

The drums I had noticed out of the corner of my eye when I first entered the camp, with a grownup pushing me on with his baton and my thumbs bound together with wire behind my back. They were lined up on either side of the road, hanging on chains, about a meter and a half from the ground. They were old oil barrels, and despite the rust you could still make out the name of the company that used to exploit the coastal fields: the five blue letters T O T A L were visible about a meter above the ground.

Hoarse moans emerged from these metal rib cages full of holes. The guards, recruited from the grownups, would pour soup in from the top, standing on their trucks and opening the drum lids, obliging the prisoners to lick the food off the insides of their jail.

Twice a day a guard would spray the captives with a garden hose, and they would drink directly from the jet. Punishment drums were changed only once a week, so that those confined there lived crouched in their own excrement.

Often these drums became coffins. When a prisoner died, grownups would close the lid tight and toss the drum into the river or into a nearby bog.

The drums were jack o'lanterns of death, monstrous low-hanging metal fruit. Occasionally a drum would emit a groan. But it was especially when one fell silent that a dull anxiety spread through the camp. That was when death was inscribed on the children's faces. "Death" was the collective term under which the names of those who had been punished were grouped and disappeared forever.

Every morning the camp warden held a roll call by striking the bottom of each drum with his club. At that moment some drums responded with a strangled cry. Sometimes in the course of a day a boy driven mad would begin to scream.

"Here he is. We brought him back alive. We caught up with him on the other side of the hill."

The grownup stayed by the door, his rifle pointed at the middle of my back.

"Untie him," commanded the Director. "You want a cigarette, boy?"

I wanted that cigarette desperately, but I told him no, not wishing to accept the slightest favor from the man.

The Director was short. His black glasses made his lips the focus of his face, lips tightly clamped to a cigarette holder that he chewed on all the time. His olive-green shirt was buttoned up to his throat. He carried no weapon. His voice, hampered by a speech defect, was high-pitched and seemingly not fully broken.

"How old are you?"

"Twelve, sir."

"If you know how, write your name in this notebook," he said, turning towards the window.

The hut to which I was escorted had no door. It had a clean cement floor with a blanket spread out in a corner.

"If you want to come out or ask for anything, stand to attention in the doorway with your hands behind your back and wait for a guard to notice you."

I used to sit inside on the blanket all day long. A little before nightfall, a loudspeaker would summon us to eat. We got soup just once a day, composed chiefly of sweetcorn and potatoes. The guards led us with our hands on our heads to a large stockpot where other children were already queueing up. We had to eat standing, quickly, and in silence.

Ahead of me on my first day was a village boy who must have been my age. We caught each other's eye right away. When the head guard whistled to indicate that mealtime was over, the boy slipped a piece of bread under my shirt.

What became of my brother and sister after I lost them in the turmoil? Did they make it to the caves behind the white cliffs?

Our house was in the riverside district two kilometers from the railroad. On that day, because we forgot to put the bread on the table, my uncle, as usual, said, "Be careful, the table might collapse." The table was the center of the house: it was for playing dominoes, for eating, for learning to read and write, for listening to the radio, and sometimes we even slept on it. In fact the table was our house within the house.

When they blocked off the street, my father was making the coffee and had just put his cigarette out in the watering can. My sister was crouched on the floor reading the newspaper.

I was thinking now of my sister, and of my mother who had

left clutching her sewing box and hiding the house key under a rock as she always did.

We all lost sight of one another after the soldiers opened fire down the street.

The day after my arrival in the camp, a grownup tossed me a puppy taken from its mother in the police kennels.

I have always loved dogs.

His reddish coat was silky and warm. He licked me with his little tongue then started nibbling my hand. I held him close and felt his heart beating. I could see that he was shivering with cold and fear, so I opened my shirt and put him directly in contact with my skin. He stopped trembling then. He poked his head out of my shirt and looked up at me. Something infinitely timeless and sweet invaded me. I hugged him even more tightly and got the feeling that I was his mother now.

This was the first moment of joy I had shared with another living being since entering the camp. I had become Dog's mother and I would softly sing him a lullaby whenever I returned to my hut. Dog was soon my sole companion and at all hours he would be entangled with my legs as though I had grown a second pair of feet.

With others I had been assigned the job of cleaning up the northern part of the camp. This gave me an odd freedom and I circulated at will among the barracks to which other children with different chores were confined.

I felt the hate-filled and threatening gaze of the grownups – to whom I was not allowed to speak – as it bore into my back after I passed by. The grownups had fully mature dogs and were responsible for keeping discipline in the entire camp.

There were two kinds of soldiers: those who remained in a watchtower next to the Director's office and those who patrolled on the far side of the barbed-wire fence and occasionally threw us cigarettes.

Dog was especially fond of fetching. I had taught him to play without making a sound, as per regulations. Whenever a grownup was approaching, Dog warned me with a growl and came and nuzzled my feet. I would always keep some sweetcorn for him to eat, for dog owners were entitled to a little extra soup.

I slept with him. We kept each other warm.

One morning, about two months after I entered the camp, the Director sent a grownup to get me. In his office he asked me right away how my charge was. Dog gamboled between our legs, then lay down on my shoes, trembling.

The Director stroked him a little, then suddenly rose, picked up a folder from the table, and opened it briskly.

"Tell me if you recognize anyone in these photographs," he said, leaning down to pet my dog once more.

He showed me one set of black-and-white identification photos – faces battered by beatings and torture – and another set of pictures taken in the street. Some of the faces were those of the dead. I turned the pages of the folder slowly, and on the third page I recognized Sando and a cripple from my neighborhood, then I came upon my father and my sister, whom I had lost sight of after the raid.

"If you recognize someone, please tell me," said the Director, chewing on his empty cigarette holder.

Dog licked the Director's hand and whined as he nipped at the heavy rings on the man's fingers. I kept on turning pages, until in one column I recognized my big brother who had disappeared up into the mountains much earlier.

"No one you know?" the Director asked me again.

"No, sir, I don't recognize anyone."

"Take a good look, you have plenty of time."

I also recognized Santiago and Roberto, and all my friends from the neighborhood, as well as participants at a meeting we had held in aid of prisoners' families. I wondered how they had managed to get a picture taken inside our house. The Director was still playing with Dog, patting him and holding his paws and having him dance.

"You still don't recognize anyone?"

"No, sir, I don't recognize anyone."

It was at that moment that I heard Dog moan. A prolonged and pain-filled wail as if he was being strangled. I turned quickly and saw that the Director had grabbed Dog by one of his paws. He had wrapped his leash around his muzzle and, keeping him bound in this way, was methodically thumping him against the wall. Everything around me began to swirl. I felt the saliva dry in my mouth but managed to croak:

"Leave my dog alone, sir."

"Do you recognize anyone in the folder?"

I did not reply. Dog's body was now making resounding thuds against the table. Nothing around me was stable.

The Director dropped Dog like a sack of potatoes. Blood was still flowing from his muzzle and making puddles on the floor.

"Here," the Director told me, holding out a basin and a rag, "you can clean him up afterwards, but first show me who you recognize in the folder."

Trembling, I pointed out my brother and my sister and then my father.

"You know where we can find them?"

I gave him the address of our house in the country, telling myself that after all by this time they must surely have left there and gone to join the others up the mountain.

"Good. Now go and take care of your dog and take the folder

—

with you. Tomorrow you'll tell me who else you recognized tonight."

I left with Dog in my arms. The battering against the wall had crushed his ear and his muzzle was still bleeding. I washed him with water, then went back to my hut behind the latrines and fell asleep with him on the floor.

That night I had a dream. A bird came down from the sky and was trying to get into a house through the roof. Then the bird took on the face of my mother and human hands grew at the end of its wings to take hold of me. Had Mama died?

Also that night I heard scratching just outside. At first I thought it was a dog. But then I recognized Pablo, from the hut next to mine. Breaking the standing curfew, he had come over for news of Dog. He had brought him a lump of sugar that the soldiers had given him. I was happy to have Pablo there.

Pablo told me that the grownups who policed us had been arrested like us in town. It was they who beat and tortured the boys in the camp cellars. Although I had never been tortured myself, while cleaning up the camp I had frequently seen grownups forcing other children to go down into the basement of a cabin at the edge of an old quarry. Once I had heard screams coming from a ventilator there.

Because there were a good many dogs, there was a rule against dog fights, and every boy with a dog had to keep it from barking. It was odd to see those trained animals walking noiselessly alongside the boys down the paths of the camp.

The Director had perfected his method. To each boy whom he selected as a future guard, he entrusted a puppy. The child was supposed to feed it and have it sleep with him. Then, after a month or two, he forced the child to torture the animal, and later to kill it. This was how he prepared future grownups to torture children to make them talk.

The next day, as I was sweeping my cell, a grownup wearing a baseball cap came to find me. In the night the wind had blown very hard and I had woken up covered with leaves.

"Stop sweeping. The Director wants to see you."

When he saw me attaching Dog by his leash to the window bars, the grownup pointed to him and added, "The Director says to bring him with you, along with the folder."

I unfastened Dog and followed the grownup. When we got near the Director's office, Dog began to whimper and tried to get away.

"Don't let your dog run off," the grownup told me.

I grabbed Dog, who was wriggling, and gathered him gently into my arms. When I entered the Director's office, Dog, recognizing the man, tried once more to flee.

"Control your dog," the Director told me, "and sit down."

At a sign from the Director, the grownup opened the door to the toilet, which was behind me.

"Turn around. Look and see who's here and what you are in for!"

I turned around. Suppressing a cry, I recognized Pablo. His face had been beaten to a bloody pulp.

"Why don't you kiss again like you did last night?" said the Director with a laugh. "That's what you get for stealing sugar."

In a split second, as in the moment before death, every detail of my encounter with Pablo the night before passed before my eyes. As if a waterfall were cascading down from a cliff and I had the power to photograph every individual drop of water. I saw his hands on my head and the kiss that we had exchanged. Pablo was chained to the window bars and bleeding from his mouth.

"You see, we were forced to deal with your friend. You both knew full well that it was forbidden for prisoners to talk and communicate with one another. We know everything that goes on here."

Then the Director asked the grownup to hit Pablo as hard as he could across his back. The grownup hit him with his baton for long minutes without letting up until he was too tired to continue. A smile briefly curled the corner of the Director's mouth, slightly stretching a scar discernible behind his eyeglasses.

"If you want him to stop, hit your dog. Show that you are a man. You have to choose. It's your pal or the dog."

I was rooted to the spot by the table, clutching Dog close against me.

"Look," the Director went on, "we're going to break one of this fairy's arms. Go on, do it," he said to the grownup, who was laughing.

Pablo began to scream as his arm was twisted.

"If you don't want him to break your sweetheart's arm, you must break your dog's leg."

Pablo started screaming again.

A terrible cry turned into silence in my throat. I realized that I had no choice, that I had to do what I was told to save Pablo's arm. I felt that I did not exist and that Dog was just a piece of wood.

The pain a dog feels is just like that felt by a human being. Sometimes both cry out in the same way. But I did not hear the shriek of my dog. A piece of wood does not cry out.

"That'll do," said the Director. "Now you are a man. Go and take care of your dog if you can."

I went outside into the yard without daring to look at Pablo still chained to the window.

The sun blinded me and lit up the monstrous metal fruit hanging from the line of trees. I was no longer thinking of the

—

piece of wood in my arms. I took Dog by his hind legs and killed him with a single blow, smashing his head down on the pavement. I went back to my hut and vomited on the spot where I used to sleep with him. I was suddenly filled with a great hatred for Pablo, for because of him I had killed Dog. Then I continued to retch but I could not bring anything up.

That night I heard pebbles being thrown onto the tin roof of the hut. Two pebbles on the left of the roof and another over the window. It was Pablo signaling. The hate vanished then from my heart, but I continued to weep at the thought of Dog.

As I held Pablo close in the darkness I felt that I was also holding my dog. They were both dead in their fashion, together, and something else, something new, had come to life. But I too was dead. In Pablo's arms I felt Dog's warm body and in my tears I confused the two. But we did not know who was the dead one, or which of us was alive. Dog was breathing like a ghost. That night, after Pablo left, a few hours before daybreak, I decided to escape.

Letting myself be carried along by the current, I swam towards the pebble beach on the far bank.

The oil drum nearest me had released its corpse. In the middle of the river a whirlpool dragged us down. I managed to escape it and then I was carried very swiftly downstream in the direction of the dam. The grownups had spotted me swimming and made an about-turn in their truck. At the river's bend, just before the rapids, they began firing at me. But by the time I reached the beach I was out of their sights.

I knew that on their return to the camp they would not say a word because they were themselves afraid of being put into punishment drums. The dead body of the boy who had been with me in the drum was floating downstream, and the grownups had now opened fire on it in the belief that he was still alive. They seemed to be playing a game.

I waited for the truck to leave. Then I headed up the mountain.

From above, the river was no longer moving, but lay stretched out like a black ribbon leading towards the sea.

Morse Code

FLORIDOR PUIG AND CHUCHO HILERO the schoolteacher had been friends since the long winter strikes which brought them together in the back room of a bar where they played their first game of chess. Every Saturday after that, in the botanical garden, the two of them constructed disjointed and melancholy games. The history, or rather the legend of Floridor Puig and Chucho Hilero is indissolubly linked to the history of drunkenness and the time-honored moves of pieces on the chessboard.

Floridor Puig was a formidable chess player, brooding and precise. Even as a boy, he used to play in the evenings with his father on a plank on which he had meticulously drawn lines with a hot iron and with chessmen carved from corks. Later on, he made chess sets by cutting up tin cans.

Everyone recalls his remarks to his comrades, who had lost the Civil War, when he spoke of another war that they still had to wage against themselves.

"You have your enemy under your shirts," he loved to say.

Floridor was also a poet and a schoolteacher. After his first arrest he drew a chessboard on the wall of his cell, which made it easier for him to explain the movements of the pieces to his fellow inmates. Even the turnkey learned the rules of the game by watching through the peephole. The soldiers who had arrested him knew his reputation as a poet and teacher. Several of them had even sat on the benches in his class at the local primary school.

It all began when in a cell that held over sixty prisoners the drum that served as a latrine needed to be emptied: "One drum for sixty! Think of the smell!" Floridor said to me.

He was the one who volunteered.

"Look! The poet is emptying the shit!" said the soldiers. "Now recite us some poems!"

Floridor recited a poem, and the next morning he gave his first collective chess lesson to prisoners and soldiers alike.

The prisoners were not always the ones who appeared to be the prisoners, Floridor said.

The arrest of the two friends came after the coup d'état that shook the country. The pair, ever committed to their dream of human emancipation, founded a resistance group called the King's Bishops. At night they scrawled quotations from Victor Hugo, Confucius, or Anarchys the Greek on the walls of their town.

The flappy ears of the swarms of informers in the area and the draconian repression of clandestine activity forced these activists to change their names. Proudly, and quite naturally, they assumed

—

73

as patronymics the names of great chess players of the past. For them History had become a vast network of hope in which pawns, bishops and knights set out to conquer kings.

Thus, for a few months, Floridor bore the name of the twelfth-century vizier Merciliad, who according to legend played with living people as chessmen in his gardens. Chucho for his part went by William Spencer, champion of the blindfold chess tournaments so common at seventeenth-century German fairs. For a whole season, braving the curfew, the two comrades continued to post manifestos on walls.

Inevitably, during one of their nocturnal sorties, as they were daubing a graffito on the façade of the town hall, the whole group was arrested. Incarcerated in the fortress overlooking the market, Floridor and Chucho were placed in individual cells on different floors.

This deliberate separation of the two by the penitentiary administration quite failed, however, to keep them from their beloved pastime. Floridor, from the third floor, and Chucho, on the ground floor next to the kitchens, continued to play games as invisible as they were loud by adopting noise-making strategies whose rhythms would have been the envy of many a percussion section.

As was traditional, the prison administrators, in order to humiliate them, had placed the pair among the common criminals, who treated them with a mixture of respect and fear. For some, Floridor was still the "schoolmaster" whose implacable moral rectitude they well remembered. During the exercise period, they all greeted him ceremoniously: "Good morning, Professor! It looks like a beautiful day. Last night we heard the nightingale sing."

During the exercise period the other prisoners addressed each of them in the polite plural form as though he was a multitude. Even the soldiers guarding them allowed themselves no loose language out of respect for the pair's reputation.

Floridor and Chucho seemed to come, moreover, from a secret, inaccessible dimension where the mysterious powers of several worlds were in play. On the chessboard, Florio and Chucho themselves envisioned our world here below, in great detail, as black and white squares separating the paths that bound them together.

So it was that every night Floridor and Chucho practiced the psycho-geometrical art of strategy. With ears pressed to the pipes, chessboard perched on the toilet, and spoon in hand, they played in Morse code like the drummers of a universal music: queenside and kingside castlings, en passant capture, Sicilian defense, counter-gambits, Italian game, Scotch game, reversed West Indian defense. In this prison guarded by a battalion of sailors of the Sixth Army, strategy became the inmates' chief object of study.

The entire prison listened to these nocturnal chess games in a spirit of worshipful reverence. At night everyone appreciated the acumen on display and the implied homage to popular resistance.

No one dared sleep. The resonating pipes broadcast a kind of tom-tom of hope from invisible and occult constellations. Freedom was playing its music and the musicians invented notes they had never before known.

Having conceived a fondness for Floridor and Chucho, the prison guards enforced silence, and as long as these strange prisoners were playing it was forbidden to relieve oneself or even open a faucet for a drink of water. Everyone restrained themselves or refrained from pulling the chain so as to give full rein to the brilliance of the captive maestros. The prison's plumbing was a conduit for an odd free jazz of sacred poetry.

Dash-dash-dot, dot, dot-dash dot, dot dash, resounded the pipes. Dash-dash dot, dot, dot-dash dot, dot dash.

Like cathode and anode, Floridor and Chucho lit a black light in the night whose brilliance everyone heard with their ears likewise pressed tightly against the pipes.

The ritual never changed within the prison's small eternity. Each player would cover the black hole of his cell's privy with a chessboard and line up the chessmen carved in cork. Every night a joust of giants was engaged between two virtual armies.

"They are going to begin!" The cry would go up, and everyone, lying on their palliasse, got ready to listen to the dull and sharp sounds of a strategy of which they understood nothing but by whose means the fate of the world, and, obscurely, their own, would be decided in the pipes.

The honor of mankind was beating out the rhythm of eternity in the prison of History.

Not long before they escaped, Floridor and Chucho each had a seahorse tattooed on their left wrist. Floridor's was white, Chucho's black.

For a long time Floridor would not explain the meaning of this tattoo to me. One evening, however, and quite by chance, as I looked at the board at the end of a game, I noticed that the only pieces still standing in the middle of the board were the knights. The game had clearly been played with the deliberate intention of not sacrificing any knights. Only then did I learn the meaning of the tattoos on their wrists.

"You see, the knight is the only piece in the game of chess that comes out of the sea and moves like its marine counterpart, the seahorse: both sideways and forwards. In life, if you don't want to fall down and you want to avoid an obstacle, move like the knight."

It was not the ordinary knight that the master was talking about, but the higher, Platonic knight of his shadow play.

A step sideways and a leap ahead: real human beings could

—

be identified by tracks left in this manner. The inventors of the game of chess hailed from a civilization lost in ships' graveyards. A horseman having his mount dance upon the earth was also having it ascend vertically with the freedom of the hippocampus in the sea.

Who deserved to belong to this secret hippocampian society and have a seahorse tattooed on their wrist? The knight was the key to the earthbound game because it came from another, marine chessboard purer than death. Focusing play on the knights was a dance that evoked a memory jealously guarded in the depths of the earth.

After that game whereby the two friends revealed the meaning of their tattoos to me, they drank, as usual, more than was in the bottles they emptied. Their eyes brimmed with invisible hypotenuses, fragrant strategies, holy wars, encircled queens and bishops, and declined gambits. Floridor threw his arm around Chucho's shoulders and, staggering like a pair of seahorses exiled on land, they headed for the garden, just then surrendering the sun to the night.

A lurch sideways and a lurch forward – thus, just like Neptune's sacred horses, they tottered to the seashore.

Drunks also move like seahorses and like knights on the chessboard. The two comrades did not wait for sleep to come: they were sleep itself. They were beyond death, they were the sea.

—

Gently, noiselessly, I lay down beside them. The two masters were sleeping, their chests rising and falling in a childlike rhythm governed by the alcohol of the last stars, when a furious wind from the depths of the sea suddenly got up and stirred not a few boats.

When I opened my eyes the sun was high in the sky and the gulls could no longer sport with it. Floridor and Chucho were still snoring fit to rival the bells of San Subra, which had started to sound the Ave Maria of the High Mass, so scorned by that the partners.

I told myself, closing my eyes, that this was how I loved mankind. I began to take a long piss into the sea. As if I were using a pencil, I wrote my name in the waves. Afterwards, it seemed to me that the sea was bigger. I had not been pissing, but filling the sea. The sea never knew it.

I took two steps forward and one sideways. Throwing myself full-length on the sand, I closed my eyes so as not to see the sky.

Chess and Beauty

SO IT WAS that in prison, then in the resistance, and now in their newfound freedom, Floridor and Chucho, regular as clockwork at five in the afternoon, like a corrida, played chess. The evening breeze would refresh their dreams along with all the memories that came from infinity like prophecies looking into the past.

Once free once more, the two friends had replayed every game and invented all possible games: the cubic game in which all the pieces can move vertically as well as horizontally; circular and spherical chess; blindfold and simultaneous variants, and so on. Voracious readers, they had even devised a literary form of chess in which they assigned a verse to each piece and to each move. At the end of each game, by combination, a poem was composed which they committed to memory and recited to each other on bleak evenings with the window open onto the mountains that dominated the town. They kept their eyes closed, and the poem turned back into a great chessboard and faithfully retraced the inexorable evolution of their game.

The knight was behind the queen
And on the rook the poppy bloomed

The pawn was thirsty in the column
where the bishop was splitting his sides

"No need to choose between love and play," Floridor would say. "Those who play at love will always know how to play the game, and those who love to play can always love."

Playing chess had become a higher form of clarity amid the randomness of the stars, of which we are the shadows or at times the imperfect numbers of their cumulation.

Light versus dark. Dark versus light. Straight, diagonal or jumping. But without hope. For equilibrium does not imply hope; if it did, hope's copper weight would outweigh all comers in its ineluctable scale. The combat between dark and light is an everlasting struggle beyond both light and night. Winning a game in History means knowing how not to win it.

"Our defeats," Floridor liked to say, "are greater than their victories."

For Floridor the game of chess was the grid of that endless combat. Everyone knows that true chess players must have no hope, otherwise they will lose any future. Hope is the ultimate prison, and the checkerboard is the first free prison where humans play on a par with the gods, because the world was created through play. But the enduring secret goal of the two comrades was to create a game whose outcome would be the rules of that game, or, in a word, beauty.

Attracted by the beauty of death, Floridor, now an old man, had decided that winning a game no longer interested him. Thereafter this champion, capable of playing on several boards at once, proceeded to lose all the games from which he would once have easily emerged victorious over his adversaries.

People said that Floridor had changed and that his legendary powers of concentration had vanished along with his strategic obstinacy. There were even some children who came to his door to goad him, and, sad to say, he would lose in front of them and beneath the barbs and facile mockery of passing amateurs.

And yet a few grand masters and the handful of loyal friends he still had left continued playing regularly with Floridor in his courtyard, away from all prying eyes.

What intrigued me over many months was the deference paid to Floridor, which I noticed whenever I happened to witness those intimates' farewells to him in front of his house at dawn: "Thank you, Maestro, what a great lesson you gave us tonight by immobilizing your king amidst Black's pieces when everyone had given you up for lost!"

I could not help wondering why these incontestably great players wasted their time measuring themselves against a man who could no longer focus his attention and let his pieces be stolen like a beginner at checkers. Was it out of friendship, pity, or compassion, or out of respect for Floridor's past virtuosity? Fascinated by this puzzle, I faithfully attended the wine-soaked gatherings in his cellar until one day I received the signal honor of an invitation to the secret sessions he held with his illustrious friends.

I have to admit that for the longest time I understood nothing and would fall asleep before a game was decided, continuing to attribute the congratulations offered by winners to a sort of condescension, or even to a simple compassion extended to a former master who had lost his mind. But one afternoon, after my usual stroll, I finally managed to disentangle the true secret of that old master's play.

I had paid a surprise visit to Floridor, who, as often, was in his garden playing against someone unknown to me. After the start and continuation of a classic game, during which Floridor violently attacked and ruptured the rank of pawns arrayed against him, I saw him refrain from capturing the queen and instead take an insignificant pawn. Between a queen and a pawn, no player would normally hesitate. But Floridor had passed up the queen without evoking any apparent reaction from his adversary, who was perhaps used by now to Floridor's new obsessions as a player.

On that day, as the game drew to its end and as Floridor, driven by a mad inconsistency, headed towards defeat, I was standing up and looking down over the chessboard when I noticed that in the center Floridor's pieces now formed the outline of a woman's face.

The king and queen were the two eyes, a line of pawns the mouth, and a knight the nose, while the two bishops stood guard over the ears like dangling earrings. The general outline of the face was supplied by the adversary's pieces on the march towards the king and his imminent checkmate.

I was flabbergasted. That night I fully grasped the nature of the old master's higher game – which everyone, out of ignorance, subjected to ridicule – and understood the enthusiasm that motivated his covert team in their search for a new conception of the game of chess.

Floridor did not want to win for winning's sake, because his strategic goal was above all to create beauty. What good was the death of the bull if the choreography of the corrida was second-rate or bungled?

So it was absolutely not simply a matter of putting the king in check, as in the secular game. It was necessary that the path leading to the death of the king should be of an impeccable rigor and beauty, and that this principle should apply to one's own king likewise.

For defeat ought to be as beautiful as triumph. The honor of death in chess was as fundamental as victory. Knowing how to lose was as noble as knowing how to win. The value of the game lay not in the glorification of the speed and effectiveness of the winner but rather in the artistry of either the defeat or the victory.

In this higher realm of the game, the one who lost often received more plaudits than the winner, for his death had been morally and aesthetically superior to any victory.

To kill or to kill oneself: no difference.

Not long after the night when I saw the image of a woman's face on the chessboard just prior to the death of the king, the old master and his friend Chucho allowed me to take part in the work of their secret society, whose headquarters was the spacious cellar beneath a bar in San Subra. It was there, in this dark temple, that the aesthetic principles of a rite invented and destroyed in every game were exposed with great intensity.

In the cellar of that bar, which we called The World, once the doors were firmly closed, these chess-loving comrades arranged their men on wooden tables and planned games of a spiritually superior kind.

In the eyes of Floridor's secret society, the winner was the player who conducted the purest campaign. And in the euphoria of our ceremonies we allowed the game to be the winner, very often celebrating two winners, both victor and vanquished, inasmuch as it was indeed the game itself that won and not the players, whom the game from a great height manipulated with strings hidden up the sleeve of eternity.

"Beauty is a double of madness. For chess may be played with the method of love or with the method of death. Tournaments are always tournaments of death. And so, my son, if you play do not try to win but seek the pure game that will let you witness the emergence of a form. Losing can be winning. Winning is merely the first step in initiation into the game. True masters know that winning is an illusion to which even children may attain. The true player, who no longer plays, pursues other goals in a quest for the truth of the game."

The Arrest

THEY CAME TO arrest me at my house, behind the railway station.

The network in which I was active had been assigned the task of forging papers. I used to make identity cards with the most official-looking rubber stamps purloined by another network member from police headquarters. Half of my work involved the alteration of documents stolen in cafés or pickpocketed in the street; the other half, which paradoxically required less effort, consisted in the creation of complete credentials from scratch. I worked in my cellar with a kerosene lamp and a miniature printing press.

In my view, making a fake document is not a form of deception but a way of entering another space. Starting from names found on gravestones or in birth and death records, I would bring an unknown person to life. My false papers were created from the names of the dead. I believe that the dead are not dead, as is generally supposed, but keep us on our feet by holding tight to our legs.

At the graveyard I would pick tombs whose epitaphs had worn away. My false papers thus became passports for the living. A password, so to speak, between those who were dead and those yet to come alive. It made me happy to think that a dead person would be fighting alongside us against the enemy. That was my interpretation of resurrection. I was putting ghosts into circulation.

True, the neighbors' dog had barked. A warning, a danger signal, is not part of a rational system, but we sense danger, often before it arises, when it is near. Who knows how much energy is mobilized by danger in realms unseen? This time, though, I heard nothing. I was thinking about the approaching end of the war. Happiness may put you to sleep in dire situations but anxiety always remains as a reservoir of lucidity. Peace is blind because it forgets that life is a balance board – a never-ending, never-resolved contest.

It was when I saw a woman watching me by my kerosene lamp that I realized that I was surely going to be betrayed. My inept claim that I was printing labels for my bottles of wine was quite inadequate. Two days later my house was raided and my clandestine workshop discovered. I let myself be led away, putting up no resistance as soldiers carted off my counterfeiting equipment.

I was thrown onto the concrete floor of a bathroom. Every morning two men came to take me out for interrogation. I recognized one of them, a former messenger boy who had opened a flower shop in the neighborhood. I also recognized the house of a trade-union lawyer who had been arrested two years earlier.

I had never been in his house, but I was shaken to see men in white shirts with rolled-up sleeves occupying it. His books, once visible from the street, had disappeared from the library along with the pictures. Now only the chandelier continued to shed its light; it occurred to me that light was neutral and could illuminate anything at all.

To ask a question is to understand the answer. A question mark is a rearing snake that bites every answer to death. A question's strength is attack; an answer's strength is defense. The challenge, therefore, is to respond in an interrogative way. Every response must itself turn into a snake.

I refused to answer their questions. I simply stated that a man unknown to me would leave in my mailbox a photo and the address of the person for whom I was supposed to forge papers. I did not say how I used to look for names in the graveyard, nor that I found the day and month of dates of birth in the annals of the great freedom fighters of our world.

When I finished a job, I told them, I would hang a bedsheet in my garden along with a pair of pants. If the pants were to the left of the sheet, it meant that the work was done and that I would put the papers under the pot of flowers facing the street. Whether it was the milkman who picked them up, or the newspaper man on his bike, or a roadworker, I never knew. I told them nothing. I gave no names.

Something inside me, beyond pain or hope, chose not to talk. I said *no*, so to speak, in order to exist.

A *no* older than the universe. A sign of creation set against the void. But a *no* beyond *yes* and *no*. A negation from a sense of honor greater than us. I did not talk.

Every morning, in the interrogation room next to the bathroom, I was bolted to a rack and immersed in a tub. When I was lifted out the water was red. This went on for three weeks.

Then came a morning when I was thrown into a railroad car with about a hundred comrades. My friend Saez had managed to conceal a file, a rat-tail round file, beneath the truss he wore as a disabled person. That file was our one and only hope. We both smiled, and at the beginning of the journey we talked about the number of tools named for animals: *herminette* (stoat) for an adze; *chèvre* (goat) for a hoist; and *pied-de-biche* (deer's foot) for a crowbar. We wondered whether it was animals who taught humans how to labor. Inside the car we took turns sitting down. We also took turns pissing through the gaps between the floorboards onto the railbed below.

With a few others, I resolved to escape, but many comrades were afraid. They pointed out that there were soldiers watching us on either end of the car's roof. The prisoners' eyes were bright with their secret hope of surviving. I knew that hope could trump survival. I also realized that hope never abides by a majority view and that, and, just like freedom, it is independent.

So, despite the handicap of our small number, we decided to escape. There were some who sought to prevent this, trying to convince us of the hopelessness of our initiative. A scuffle ensued, and we had to fight to facilitate our escape. I don't enjoy recounting this episode in the rail car, because it still pains me to say that I fought some of my own who were under the illusion of being alive.

It was hard to believe that the spirit of the enemy was manifesting itself in our car. The enemy was almost right there among us. Our comrades, without wishing to, had allied themselves with our captors. To attempt escape we now had to see them as enemies. Not completely, however. Those comrades were provisional enemies only: I realized that you have to know how to fight those who do not want to free themselves in order to make their liberation possible.

The railroad car had served to transport cattle. It stank of liquid manure and straw. I reflected that we were cattle also, but that what made us different from cattle was the basis of our hope. Not survival. Cattle no more want to die than most of the comrades in that car did. The difference between cattle and us was that even if we could not avoid each other, we could escape.

It is not our ability to speak or to string words together that makes us different from cattle but the fact that we ally those words with something that words know nothing of. So long as speech does not embody hope it is no more than bellowing.

We fought with our own and then I made a hole in the car's door. One of us reached his arm outside and undid the bolt. A few minutes later, as the train slowed down on a bend, we all threw ourselves out and tumbled into a ravine. The soldiers on the car's roof fired at us but we were already far away and under cover of rocks and trees.

Here for your consideration are a few lessons I learned that day:

First, the struggle to escape from a railroad car often begins among the passengers and not by engaging the soldiers guarding the transport, because a good number of those passengers are unaware of their degree of confinement.

Secondly, hope is a hole made in the side of a rail car.

Thirdly, any captive passenger in the car must invent a new, impossible way out of the car as opposed to the possible one.

Fourthly, those who remained in the car and did not wish to escape were, nevertheless, shot.

The White Library

IN A SHOP WINDOW I saw a red book with gold lettering. *The History of the Universe* was its title. I asked Mama to buy it for me, but she couldn't, because she had no money and my dad had not yet come back from the other side of the mountain. So every night I said a prayer, as the neighbor lady had told me to do, and every morning I looked under my bed to see if the book had arrived. But no. Not under the wardrobe either, nor with the shoes. Finding nothing under the bed but an endless accumulation of white dust bunnies made me give up praying.

Maybe prayer failed to bring me the book because it was no longer in the shop window and more than likely already sold.

I had prayed scrupulously for that book. But praying clearly did not work miracles of that sort. It simply couldn't cause a book to appear under my bed. God was not Santa Claus. Telling the rosary had no effect at all.

Everyone in the neighborhood said that there was a man living on the edge of the village who had a library.

One evening as he was leaving the café I managed to meet him. They said he was a professor or even a monk. I hesitated to call him Professor because he really seemed to walk like a monk. But

---

then I called him Professor like everyone else. I went up to him just as he was coming out.

"Professor," I said, "I've been told that you have a library. Please, sir, would you show it to me?"

The man began to laugh and asked me why. I replied that I had never seen a real library. I was afraid of being afraid but not of the man. Still laughing, he led me to his house.

He lived in one room. Part of his bed was under the dining table. The dishes in the sink were inches from his pillow. Despite the disorder, the room was all white. At first I wondered where the books were. I couldn't see any. But soon enough I got the idea: I really was in a library but you could not immediately see the books lining the walls. They were all standing the wrong way round, and what you took for the color of the wall was in fact the whitish hue of their fore-edges.

The professor had arranged his books with their spines to the wall. It was rather like turning a painting or photograph over. No titles, no authors' names, no series indications, just petrified white horses on a sea by an ancient spray-swept beach.

On the shelves, themselves painted off-white, all that could be seen was an endless procession of white streaks undulating like a dirty snow field. The professor did not want anyone to know what he was reading. Perhaps authors' names and titles distracted him from writing his own books. Perhaps that was why he turned the volumes around. But how could you find a particular book on the shelves? The professor clearly possessed thousands of books. I asked him how he managed to distinguish them.

"I know them all," he replied, running his fingers over a rank of back-facing tomes as if it was a piano keyboard. "You will get to know them too. I'm going to teach you. Before you read a book you have to be acquainted with it. Only after that do you read. Come back tomorrow. I'll teach you."

Tomorrow came. Following his instructions, I turned a shelf's worth of books around. The titles meant nothing to me, but I liked them. The professor had not arranged his books by author's name but by title. He had a notebook, likewise all white, in which he had listed all the authors and titles. For example:

Zhuanzi, *The Inner Chapters*
Simone Weil, *Awaiting God*
Alain, *Twenty Lessons on the Fine Arts*
Husserl, *The Crisis of European Humanity and Philosophy*
Kant, *Treatise on Education*
Althusser, *The Solitude of Machiavelli*
d'Alembert, *Conversation between Descartes and Christina
    of Sweden*
Anaximander, *Fragments*
Aristotle, *Nicomachean Ethics*

The professor had me learn the titles by heart. Every day I learned a new title and a new author. Every evening, when I went back to his house, I would recite them to him. And at the end of each week he would get me to recite all the titles and authors of the past seven days. When I went by after school he would have replaced all the books, back to front, on his shelves.

Although at the outset he had me recite authors and titles in this way, little by little he began to call them out himself, and I was expected to find specific books in their places against the wall solely from their fore-edges.

I was a quick study. The professor was very pleased. He told me that I too would become a philosopher. One morning he directed me to the tenth shelf:

"Get me *Conversations on the Plurality of Worlds*."

I scrutinized the white fore-edges of the books on the tenth shelf and gently removed the work from the middle of the rank without making a mistake. The author was Fontenelle. But the professor was already on to his next command, as if playing a game:

"Fourier, *The Straying of Reason, as Exemplified by the Absurdities of the Inexact Sciences*."

The book was on the third shelf. I knew this. Its fore-edge was yellower than that of its neighbors. It was not cheating to have noted the fact. I took the work out and brought it to the professor. Sometimes I thought he was insane.

Two years passed. I now had the entire library in my head. I could reel off its contents and was well acquainted with its topology. The whites of the books' pages were not all of the same shade. For instance, *The Part Played by Labor in the Transition from Ape to Man*, by Friedrich Engels, had a bright white fore-edge and pages as thick as blotting paper. Nearby was Epictetus's celebrated *Manual for Living*, its pages yellow, thin and tight. As for Erasmus's *In Praise of Folly*, it had pages of a white well-nigh gray.

When it came to the white, creamy, or yellowed shading of the pages, I was like an Eskimo. To me no two whites were the same. I have read that the Inuit have forty or so different words for snow.

The professor made me create sentences out of book titles. Then poems, by linking these sentences together. I came to look on each book's fore-edge as a line in a poem.

I noticed that between every fourteenth and fifteenth volume on his shelves the professor had slipped a sheet of paper. He told me that fourteen was the number of lines in a sonnet. So I learnt what a sonnet was, and soon I was reciting Gérard de Nerval's "El Desdichado" every day. By this time I no longer needed to pull books out to know their titles, and I was able to recite titles as poems without hesitation.

Reading blind from the fore-edges aligned on the first shelf produced the following poem:

On the Unity of the Divine Trinity (Abelard)
Is a Book on The Licit and the Illicit (Al Ghazali)
And the Allegory of Poets (d'Alembert)
Is always an Unpublished Text (Alain de Lille)

Like the Book of Flowers (Sakurazawa-Ohsawa)
On the Way to Language (Heidegger)
Is a Science of Logic (Hegel)
Or An Attempt at a Critique of All Revelation (Fichte)

On the Spirit of Humanity (Von Humboldt)
Is The Art of Social Life (Lalo)
It is also a Discourse on Voluntary Servitude (La Boétie)

The Instrumental Nightingale (Ledu)
Proclaims a Reform of Dynamics (Leibniz)
With reference to The Question of Truth (Aquinas)

Now I knew the whole list of the books in the library – in order and according to shelf. Before school each morning the professor trained me like an athlete. He would call out the title of a work for me to find and immediately I would climb the stepladder and find it straight away. I had become as good at this as the professor himself.

I knew every title and every poem of the back-to-front library. I understood that a poem could be composed solely of titles. If I faltered in my recitations, it was because speaking implied combining all the titles in the world. In a poem, every verse contained a whole book.

One morning, waving at his library, the professor told me: "Now you may read."

The professor was truly crazy. His library really held only one book: the book of all the poems he had composed from his titles. That day I began slowly to read inside the books. The library was all white. The light slid over the whiteness of the books.

Outside it was snowing. I gazed at the tracks left by a dog walking down the road as though they were the sorts for a press that no one had yet invented.

The Treasure of the Spanish Civil War

THE LETTER HAD been slipped beneath the house's inevitable geranium on the windowsill. It was old María – María who repaired mattresses – who had put it there. The stamp was upside down, naturally: the sign that it was one of ours who had addressed the envelope in violet ink, in big letters with curly upstrokes and downstrokes. Pua read out his own name as if he were encountering it for the first time:

Pua Moreno
La Cadena Street
(back of courtyard next to the mattresser)
San Subra District

Pua immediately recognized the handwriting of the *Comandante*.

What does he want with me? he wondered. I haven't seen him in ten years. I heard he was net-fishing sardines near the border.

So great was Pua's respect for the written word that he jacketed all his books with newsprint. On each spine he wrote the title and the author's name with pen and ink. Then, at the base, in blue, using his Sergent-Major fountain pen, he would systematically add "Freedom Library." He gave the Penal Code and cookbooks exactly the same treatment. For Pua any actual book was an agent of liberation.

Pua slipped the envelope inside the cover of an Esperanto dictionary.

But let me tell you about Pua.

When Pua left the concentration camp he moved quite automatically to the San Subra neighborhood along the river, where the Gypsies and horse breeders lived.

Pua rarely received letters.

Opening a letter right away was beyond him, and it could often take him several days of reflection.

A letter was a rare thing indeed.

Pua pulled up the old straw-bottomed chair and poured himself a glass of wine. He sat down with his elbows on the waxed tabletop and gazed at the letter, once more noting the upside-down stamp.

It was the Comandante...

It was definitely him, he told himself for the second time. For three days Pua did not open the envelope and merely contemplated it. He went out to the local cafés, dawdled in restaurants till very late and got drunk twice in the Bar des Amidonniers before at last, on the Sunday, going to the public baths for his weekly shower.

He yelled insults against the dictator, smashed a chair, broke open some mailboxes, unchained a dog, and made a little money by sticking banknotes against the walls of certain bars with his forehead. On the third day, but only after he was properly dressed and shaved, he opened the letter.

He performed this ritual on the terrace of a café that he never frequented in a neighborhood across the river where he never usually set foot.

What did the Comandante want?

In red letters, just a few words:

I know the place. We are about to begin digging. Meet in Argelès on the anniversary of Caraquemada's death. Let the others know.... I will be waiting for you. Everyone should bring a pail and shovel. That should suffice.

Libertarian greetings.

Pua was moved to learn that the Comandante remembered the death of Caraquemada, shot down by the French police not far from the border. The letter was unsigned. But it was from him. From the Comandante.

The "place" in question was the location where some veterans of the Durruti Column had hidden part of the Republic's gold which the anarchists had appropriated from the Communists.

It had been agreed to let twenty years elapse before acting. The Comandante had kept his word.

Somewhat overwhelmed by the weight of this news, which had to be kept secret at all costs, Pua went directly to Manolo's bar. There, he knew, he would find the others: Chucho and Hilero, sitting at their chessboard between the frying pan and the pale spring sunlight filtering through the café's curtains.

"*Hola!* This is it! We're going to dig the baby up!" said Pua in a low voice.

"Baby" was the code word they used for the treasure. Chucho and Hilero interrupted their game and started to read the missive. There was no doubting it: this was the *Comandante's hand*.

The news spread like wildfire within the small circle of anarchists by the river and everyone set about preparing for the expedition.

In the compartment they were all there: Puig's son, Rico and old María, the chess players, Denis, Vásquez, and the Schoolmaster, as well as the two *compañeros* from the library. You should have been there at the station that morning to see this unlikely crew waiting for their train, then crowding together in silence on the wooden seats of third class.

A good many of the passengers on the train headed for the sea were old *Durritistas*. María had brought two large bags of provisions. Everyone had crammed their pack with wine and dry sausage and everyone carried a shovel wrapped in newspaper by their side like a soldier's rifle. The ticket inspector's suspicions must not be aroused: they all assumed that he would be in bed with the police. Loyal to the adage that "he who steals an egg will steal a cow," they were convinced that every official was a potential turnkey or informer.

Their journey, unbelievably long, was punctuated by chess games, snoring, frequent meals, and reasonable questions about the purpose of the mission.

"Do you think we'll find it?" asked Rico.

The Schoolmaster, whose words had weight, replied amid silence: "The information is solid. The Comandante has been on the spot for ten years. He had the secret location from the lips of old Liberto himself – the very one who dug the hole."

After this pronouncement in the Schoolmaster's authoritative tone the issue never came up again. It was as though any further doubts would somehow jinx the operation. The Schoolmaster, who owed this sobriquet to having trained organizers at the union, had handed out a few copies of *L'Espoir*, a paper that everyone took but nobody read – the news was always too bad; and today, as ever, the only subject was betrayals and bad turns of events.

No one slept, but at daybreak everyone had reached the rocks bordering the beach. Several hundred meters away the

Comandante suddenly came into view. While waiting for us he had already begun digging at the place they call Le Racou. Then, without a word, and without saluting him as we would have done at the Front, we all set to work, our eyes brimming with tears.

From time to time I cast a timid glance at our "hero" digging in the sand. He conveyed strength, and I was drawn to him. At the same time he frightened me a little, for once I had overheard my father burst out laughing as he told how the Comandante had killed the village priest and hung his body from the bell tower. When he smiled, I couldn't help seeing a hanged man at the end of a rope coming out of his mouth.

As our shovels delved in the sand, the ingots of the Spanish Republic awaiting us built up hopes for a temporary abolition of wage labor. It was Christmas Eve by the seaside in that spring of 1958. Everyone deserves an out-of-season Christmas once in a while.

After an hour the beach was full of holes. It was almost as though thousands of giant moles had taken up residence.

At noon the Comandante lit a fire. This was the signal for everyone to open their packs and dismantle a bicycle abandoned by history: it was an easy matter to improvise grills because the beach was right next to the dump.

Once old cardboard boxes, broken fruit crates and driftwood had been gathered it was time to get out the cutlets and *boutifarre*.

The men took care of the meat while the women made salad with tomatoes and olives and onions. Water bottles and *porrones* were passed around. We took it easy. We even kissed the Comandante; he was already completely drunk, but we forgave him.

Pua noticed flashes up on the hillside. We wondered whether we were being watched. Pua had set up an effective lookout system: whenever an intruder approached the entrance to the beach, he whistled between two fingers, at which everyone began to run around and play soccer. The only problem was that we had no ball. The players mimicked a match, and sometimes as many as three goalies would leap for an invisible ball at the water's edge.

In those days, however, there were no tourists and beaches were often quite deserted.

Pua resolved to bring a ball next time, suspecting intuitively that the recovery of the treasure might take a long time.

We took our siesta. We waited for late afternoon to resume our digging, and overnight we rolled ourselves up in blankets. Which brought back devilishly sharp memories for all those who had been imprisoned in the camp. There was talk of the war, and of the dead – and of the living, who were more dead than the dead...

The next morning we started work early, for it was Sunday and there was no time to lose. The entire day until sundown was spent digging holes. We found old barbed wire, seashells, bottles, remnants of nets, a great deal of wood, but no ingots.

A moment came, however, when the whole gang downed tools and hope flamed in everyone's eyes: Amelino's shovel had struck a crate. Ceremoniously, since it was his role, the Comandante went down into the hole and with a screwdriver popped the clasps on the box. But all that we found were old pistols probably buried during the war. That crate was nevertheless a bearer of hope: at least we had found something. The pistols showed that we were surely on the right track. We decided to leave them where they were. They might serve later. The crate was covered with sand once more.

We arranged to meet again at the same place at the end of the next week, and we swore ourselves to secrecy. Everyone went back to Toulouse with their dreams and with their lips sealed.

But, as we all know, no secret is ever well kept, and in the San Subra neighborhood this particular "secret" traveled like a lit fuse to a powder keg. On the following Saturday, when the whole team arrived with a conspiratorial air, the beach was already thronged with people. From a distance they appeared to be tourists, but as we got closer we realized that they were "diggers."

We recognized neighbors, friends, cousins. The Comandante moved forward and, after swallowing hard, silently organized digging by his following. *Because he, after all, had the map, and the others did not.*

That was obvious, moreover: some people were even delving

by the side of the road. It was a crazy scene, crazier than any beach had ever witnessed – with the possible exception of the Normandy landings. The beach of Argelès was being turned into a gigantic mole burrow. Piles of sand surrounded the holes and a small mountain had begun to grow near Le Racou. Larger and larger groups were invading the beach. Even children were to be seen busy with little buckets and spades.

A band of Gypsies from Perpignan set up camp on the fringe of the work area, and Pua, who no longer needed to serve as lookout, still retained the role of organizer of football matches. On that day, by noon, he was mustering volunteers for a knock-out competition.

Everyone came together in joyful communion, and the whole beach fraternized when it was time to eat. Siesta time suggested nothing so much as a slumbering battlefield. The sleep of the just was filled with dreams of being pirates on holiday at the seaside. So ended the second week.

But what was bound to happen happened. The next Saturday, the municipal authorities, in great alarm over the demented excavation of their beach, sent in the local police force.

The police force was a constable nicknamed *Manivelle*, or Handle, because, as was the custom also in nearby villages, his drum was beaten not with a pair of sticks but rather by means of an articulated arm mounted by the skin. By turning a handle, he was able to produce one of the finest drum rolls on the coast. He was a Communist, of course, just like the municipality itself.

After his third drum roll, Manivelle, adorned by his permanent straw hat, made a series of announcements: the program of the open-air picture show, namely *Robin Hood* with Errol Flynn and a Tarzan film with Johnny Weissmuller; a meeting at the fishermen's cooperative; the imminent visit of the butcher's van to a site behind the church; a sardana *appleg*; and the opening of subscriptions for a mammoth snail bake in two weeks' time.

Everyone listened religiously to this recitation. Then, though it was not his custom, Manivelle caused his drum to sound once more. The locals present all thought that someone must have died. They all held their breath as they waited for the bad news, but then Manivelle, after the inescapable words "Notice to the public," delivered himself of this salvo:

THE MUNICIPAL COUNCIL DECREES THAT IT IS FORBIDDEN TO DIG HOLES ON THE BEACH AND THAT ALL HOLES ALREADY DUG MUST WITHOUT EXCEPTION BE IMMEDIATELY FILLED IN. ANYONE CONTRAVENING THIS ORDER WILL BE SUBJECT TO A FINE.

To which the Comandante responded in a loud voice: "If I lay my hands on the *hijo de puta* who informed I'll bury him alive. Loose tongues always lose us the Revolution. People can't even keep a simple secret."

The fact is that the Comandante, despite his anarchist credentials, was an admirer of Blanqui with the rock-solid conviction that the triumph of liberty depended on a conspiracy against the State. He had even dreamt of tunneling under the Vatican and blowing up the Sistine Chapel. Nobody dared look him in the eye because we all knew him to be capable of the best and the worst. So we stopped digging. The beach was empty in no time.

It was noon. The scene was as bleak as the aftermath of a bombing. You might have thought that World War III had broken out on the beach at Argelès-sur-Mer. We all felt a little bit ashamed. We did not know if this was because we had created a landscape of devastation on one of France's most beautiful strands or because we had given away a secret. But many of us, clearly contrite, hung our heads.

Nevertheless, the original San Subra contingent did not give up. It was our First Attack Unit, namely Pua, who proposed a new plan to the Comandante. Some time before, he had managed to purloin a tent from the American Army: an immense marabout as big as a small-circus tent. Guy ropes and pegs were procured as well as a truck to haul it all. The Comandante settled for a new strategy: he applied to the mayor's office for permission to pitch the marquee, claiming that we were workers wishing to hold a meeting to plan for the twentieth anniversary of the concentration camp.

I don't know if the mayor believed us, but he gave us our head. Maybe he thought that he could lay his hands on the treasure once we had found it? Be that as it may, we erected the marabout at a fresh site, behind Le Racou.

As we dug in the middle of the massive tent, discreetly and in silence, we disposed of the sand by spreading it thinly across the beach. The mole had become the last animal in all creation to be found on the beach of Argelès. World War III was over. Now it was more like *The Great Escape* with Steve McQueen that was underway. It was Saturday.

On Sunday a rude surprise was in store for us. The Comandante had disappeared. Someone told us that they had seen him leave with shovel and pick. Officially, he was ill, and had needed to be transported to Varsovie Hospital in Toulouse with a stomach ailment.

In face of this latest bad luck that had befallen us, Pua, First Attack Unit, became the Comandante's legitimate successor, and as such proceeded to fill in the hole beneath the tent.

We held a meeting. We took the marabout down. We began singing. We got drunk, and everyone slept in the truck that had brought us.

—

The next day we had news of the Comandante. He was doing better. We were glad to hear it.

Apparently the treasure map with which he had been entrusted was misleading. The Comandante let us know that he now believed that we had chosen the wrong beach, and that Saint-Cyprien was where we should dig. So we got ready to move in secret from one beach to another. In any case there were too many people at Argelès, including the Gypsies encamped there and searching for the treasure without making their intentions clear.

The difference between a public secret and a private one is that the first is whispered in the ear while the second is shouted from the rooftops.

A few holes were dug at Saint-Cyprien but this new work site was soon abandoned. To this day tales of the treasure hunt are told among survivors of the Spanish War and their children. Some people talk of shifting terrain, others of the intervention of the police, of fighting with chance arrivals wanting to join the hunt, of the anti-Franco snail bakes, of sardana festivals which taught some how to keep time, of sausage-eating contests, of an attack on the town hall, of the Comandante letting himself be buried in the hole, and of his ghost wandering on stormy nights ....

Pua knew that legend trumps reality, for legend is possibility that reality cannot realize: the way to the infinity of the possible. The path to a treasure is often the treasure itself. Pua believed that what we call *the Way* is never more than a hesitation. But the most important thing is the memory of the Way, and how we transmit that memory or that way. That is what he used to say, and he was right.

Hope is always a memory of the past. Above his bed, instead of a crucifix, Pua had nailed up a battered pair of shoes. Whenever doubt threatened his hopes, he would contemplate those old black shoes, which were like the wings of a crow about to fly out through the window. Then he would tell himself, over and over: "Do not go where the road may lead. Go where there is no road, and leave tracks."

Pua said that the holes left in the beach at Argelès were the real treasure, but not everyone understood what he meant.

The Apostle of Peace

"LOOK! IT'S THE beam of peace!"

I looked up and saw the immense beam that bisected the roof of the labor exchange. A beam that ran the full length of the hall.

In those days I believed that the workers wanted to turn the world into a house of happiness. I thought that this was why, in each town, they raised a beam, for the world was wide and many beams and many halls would be needed to build their house.

But when my father said, "Look! It's the beam of peace!" his Spanish-accented French made *la poutre*, the beam, sound like *l'apôtre*, the apostle. What I *heard* was "the apostle of peace" – and there, sure enough, before us at the end of the beam, stood an imperious white-plaster bust of Jean Jaurès.

The Spanish exiles had a great veneration for the French socialist and anti-militarist, fatally shot on the eve of the Great War by an assassin prophetically named Villain. The anarchists avenged Jaurès's murder by executing Villain in Ibiza during the Spanish Civil War, and they always pronounced the victim's name with an emotional reverence.

In my town Jaurès's bust stood against a black backdrop in a hall with metal folding chairs. A red flag and a tricolor were draped around the head. Seen in profile, the plaster figure seemed to be guarding the entrance to a place where History held public meetings. At the time, the roof of the labor exchange was supported by wooden posts, since replaced by concrete columns. The enormous beam that traversed the room ended at the exact place presided over by the mute, bearded bust of the great man.

From *l'apôtre* to *la poutre* is a very small step, and only years later did I realize my mistake. It happened on a Sunday morning when I arrived early for an all-tendency anti-Franco meeting: I noticed then that Jaurès, at the end of the beam, was smiling his plaster smile.

As a boy, listening to my father, I had looked at the beam but had not followed it to its termination in the wall. A child's eye may stop looking before seeing all that is to be seen. And yet what I misheard, as a newcomer to History and on account of my father's pronunciation, was not wrong: the "apostle of peace" became a true beam, a light in the darkness of the great butchery of workers that was the First World War.

Poutre or *apôtre*, in either case Jaurès played his role to perfection, and to this day, whenever I notice his statue in public squares I picture a beam taking shape above it and dangling from it, like the two pans of a pair of scales, the two eyes of a child of exiles.

And the voice of a Spanish Republican still murmurs, in the French of his hope, *"Look! It's the apoutré of peace looking at us."*

The Bench

THIS BENCH IS a bench.

This bench is the very epitome of a bench: a long narrow wooden seat allowing several people to sit together.

This bench is a Platonic idea of a bench: all alone, gliding through the heaven of the pure ideas of all benches. A worm-eaten bench, polished and worn by generations of schoolchildren in gray smocks. A bench on either end of which you should not sit for fear of toppling off, feet in the air, to roars of laughter from infinity. A true bench, therefore. Horizontal, wobbly, lopsided – stopping-place for all wayfarers, even those who have lost their way.

This bench, on the concrete floor of the guardhouse, with a soldier sitting on it, is the matrix of all the benches in existence. But here beside the railroad line, amidst ghosts of the travel-weary and thirsty, it has become the centerpiece of a bench museum, saved long ago by some collector from the programmed elimination of all the world's benches.

The soldier has chosen his spot well. He asks me to sit, like him, at one end of the bench, so that he can watch me. When I entered the guardhouse I had seen from his reddened eyes that he was exhausted and had obviously not slept in a long while.

At his signal we both sit down at the same time, one at each end of the bench.

The nearby church bell tolls one in the morning. A police dog barks very close to the guardhouse. Despite the trains that pass regularly, the soldier has nodded off.

I have been in the guardhouse for at least two hours now, my legs hurt, and my wrists are raw from the handcuffs.

By shifting my backside, I try to find the exact point that would allow me to get to my feet without making the bench tip and above all without making the soldier slide off. The slightest false move or haste on my part might cause the soldier's weight to raise the bench and thus alert him to the fact that I have stood up. I resolve to alter my position by imperceptible increments. At each of these movements my guard instinctively corrects for the slight challenge I have made to our seat's stability.

The soldier is dreaming. He is in a huge house where an old woman walks on crutches. He opens a door. The door of an armoire. But he closes it again. He knows that behind it is the mouth of a fathomless well. Now the door opens by itself. Someone is pushing it from within. Someone is waiting for him at the bottom of the well. The soldier leaves the house. Then he realizes that he has failed to rescue the old woman on crutches. He goes back inside but the old woman has vanished. He thinks

—

that she must already have gone out through another door. He looks for her outside but does not see her. The soldier tries to walk but his legs are numb and won't let him. He knows that someone imprisoned in the well is after him, but he cannot go more quickly. Just as he is about to be caught he wakes up. He doesn't know where he is, but then realizes he is in the guardhouse. The bench has moved. The guard restores the bench's equilibrium balance and shifts his position because his legs hurt.

It occurs to the guard that his prisoner too must have legs that hurt. The guard goes back to sleep.

A fly is circling in the guardhouse. I know that I have to turn into a fly. I have to brave the storm. I have to land on dung. I have to escape through the skylight of the guardhouse. Another fly has come in. It looks at me, then changes direction. Turning my head for a split second I see that it has landed on the soldier. I must become a fly too. Flies have a freedom that we lack.

I must acquire the fly's ability to be present in two different places almost simultaneously. I must be swift and silent. I must absolutely choose to be a fly.

I see myself now soaring above the soldiers and the trains. The fly is delivering a message. The fly is a maquisard within the temporary jail where I find myself.

Outside, a noncommissioned officer is shouting orders under the rain. The same orders over and over. Then comes barking: it seems to me that the soldier marching along the railroad line has a dog on a leash. I can hear the dog panting. I can hear my guard sleeping behind me; he is snoring softly. He seems calm now. The handcuffs hurt my wrists. I wiggle my toes in my shoes. I have pins and needles. That is what we used to say as kids: pins and needles. In point of fact it is the blocking of the circulation in my thighs, the backs of which are on the edge of the bench, that is numbing my two legs. My feet are blocks of wood. I am in pain. I simply have to get up. My blood absolutely must start flowing again. Thousands of needles are pricking my feet. I raise first one and then the other shoe and tap a foot gently on the floor to get the blood moving. I have to get up at all costs and get the circulation going again, but the bench must not move.

I have no illusions about the fate that awaits me. A suspect I assuredly am. The policemen who arrested me on the train handed me over to this army unit while my papers were checked. It will not take them long to discover my real identity – before the night is out, or possibly tomorrow.

I hear the church bell tolling: the night is half over. Then another bell responds like an echo. I have heard two bells tolling almost at the same time, but there is a lag between them. Twice, three times I note this lag. Then I realize that I am myself this interval in time, this "almost" that separates the two peals. I must become an echo.

———

Should I kill this soldier in order to escape? I could, but I don't think I will. I don't want to kill the sleeping soldier. A third bell resounds as if from underground. My concern right now is to stop my feet going numb by letting the blood flow through my thighs. I lift each leg in turn and rotate my ankles. My first goal is to shift from my closed-knee sitting position at the end of the bench to a spread-legged one from which I can better control the bench's balance.

I have lucked upon a tired soldier, for despite the directives of his superior officer he has sensed my change of position but failed to forbid it. In fact his posture is just like mine.

It is a posture, however, which does not alter the fact that, should either of us stand up, the bench will inevitably tip up and clatter back onto the concrete floor.

I move my backside slowly on the end of the bench, centimeter by centimeter, raising myself up from time to time so that the bench tips down slightly at the soldier's end, unbalancing him. Regularly, still half-asleep, he corrects the balance that I have thus disturbed by almost indiscernibly moving his own rear end.

My movements toward the front of the bench are as slight and natural as those any man sitting down all night long might make to avoid cramps. The soldier is in the same situation as me. His position is likewise unstable. Since I am handcuffed, he cannot

—

possibly imagine that I might escape. So he himself shifts his backside, quite naturally, to avoid tipping up the bench.

The bench thus represents the invisible plane on which we are ensconced and which constrains us. That the soldier's own legs might fall asleep is one external disturbing factor, for example, for which I am not exclusively responsible. Quite as easily as an escape attempt on my part, the soldier's painful legs could also precipitate a fall.

The equilibrium of the bench might be considered not as a static situation but rather as a cycle, a succession of situations involving my feet, the guard's feet, and even noises and motion outside the guardhouse. The notion of equilibrium inside the guardhouse depends on a specific point of view that at once unites and separates the two of us. That point of view combines those of the bench, the guard, and myself.

The soldier has a back just like mine and fatigue just like mine. He has no wish to disturb the peace of his fragile slumber.

By now I am at the very end of the bench. I know that the soldier has moved his rump a tiny bit further along and is supporting himself on legs spread even wider. He is leaning on the barrel of his rifle: I see that, in response to my barely perceptible shifts, he has thus assumed the position of a tripod and the bench has become perfectly stable.

—

I know that the time has come to put the bench's confident balance to the test.

I decide to get to my feet, breathing from my stomach and letting the blood flow down through my legs. The tingling in my right foot makes me stumble, but I rise successfully and the bench does not tip. When I hoist myself up onto the windowsill I can see a soldier patrolling the station platform.

I decide to sit back down on the bench and wait for the next train to come through. The station is suddenly silent. I realize that this next train will be my last chance. But will it ever arrive? In the rhythm of the cars gliding along the rails you can hear whole symphonies. The ties, bolts, and track ballast, along with the cadence of the wheels, suggest so many musicians playing under the direction of an invisible conductor. Trains cannot be against me, nor can their music.

Every would-be fugitive ought to master the circus arts: aerial perch, tightrope, chair balancing, stilts, and walking globes. On this bench I am juggling horizontally with equilibrium so as not to fall. Or, perhaps better, balance is seeking its own balance so as to go on existing.

In fact the bench, the soldier, and I constitute a set of interactions that may be deemed stable just so long as no agency has an interest in changing its strategy. But should the bench no longer be at risk of tipping up even though I am standing, my strategy will have created a new equilibrium. A pendulum self-stabilized in the wake of its oscillation is said to be "in stable equilibrium." As I get to my feet I make doubly sure that the bench does not wobble.

The soldier is still sleeping, believing that I am still on the other end of the bench. But I am on my feet, behind him, contemplating his crossed hands grasping his rifle.

The bench, balanced, is not budging. I have become its extremity, detached now, and leaving through the window.

The bench was really a stilled pendulum. A motionless horizontal clock. The guard sitting on one end restored stability at each of my subtle movements. This meant that his strategy, which counted on his being woken up when he was tipped off the bench, did not work. I had calculated most carefully that the bench would not rise and clang back onto the floor when I got to my feet. Once, twice, three times I stood up, and each time the bench remained perfectly stable. Without realizing it, the guard had definitively corrected the imbalance and was now still asleep, leaning on his gun.

Outside, the rails began to quiver. A rumble caused the guardhouse floor to shake. The train I was awaiting was pulling in. The last one of the night. It was now or never. Later would be too late.

I got up slowly, and just as I had trained him to do over the last few hours, my guard, grunting, adjusted his position. I had become double. One me was still sitting at the back of the room on the bench but another me was standing before the window and heaving myself up.

I had trained the bench not to tip up and to wait for me. I had almost reached the window. The confidence filling me now was founded on the fact that I could not imagine that this was me escaping, only that I was still sitting on the bench to make sure it would not tip up.

Perhaps the one escaping was just a figment of the imagination of the one still seated? Perhaps I was just an illusion? All the same, I was on my feet and past my guard.

He was still sleeping as I pulled myself up to the window. Outside I could see the train, stopped. A compartment window was open, and opposite me was an officer, perhaps a commanding officer.

He looked at me. I did not believe that this was an officer across from me, just a man. For his part he could not believe that I was a prisoner escaping.

The officer was not there: it was someone else at the train window watching me tumble noiselessly onto the platform with my hands manacled. And it was not he who watched me cross the railroad line and go down the little path behind the station. Not he who said nothing and failed to raise the alarm. It was he, however, who, too late, fired at me. I crawled under the stationary train. Then I ran off on the far side toward the trees.

Behind me nobody moved.

—

I am thinking that we are not in a state of war. That the enemy has not bombarded the entire region. That thousands of children are not wandering the roads. I fancy that I am playing a game in winter, by the fire, drinking a glass of brandy and stuffing an old pipe.

I watch the dice rolling on the table and move my men. A game is a formal arrangement in which two or more players each decide on a strategy in the full awareness that its success depends on the choices of all. Two players, the soldier and I, chose a bench as our scales. The player who stood up first without causing the bench to tip would undoubtedly have a chance to win and leave through the window. The victor would maintain equilibrium but lose the bench. Those were the stakes. The loser would win the bench and carry it on his back his whole life long as testimony to a theory of equilibrium.

I tell myself that it is not me running through the trees but that other me sitting on the bench in the guardhouse by the station platform. But one rider on a seesaw has escaped today. I am a plaything in thrall to a mathematical law that I do not understand.

At the end of the walkway leading into the woods, which is cluttered with the trunks of felled trees, a dog barks when it sees me but then goes silent as though grasping the implications of this signal.

The guardhouse in which I was being held captive is locked with a key, and the soldier is still sitting on the bench. I know he must be awake by now. He is afraid, and raises the alarm through the window. But it is already too late. A siren blares on the platform. The other soldiers begin firing towards the forest. I am running alongside a stream. I think I recognize the trees in the forest.

Postface

Aunque me tiren en el puente
y también la pasarela
me verás pasar el Ebro
en un barquito de velas

They can shoot at me on the bridge
and on the walkway too
but you'll see me cross the Ebro
in a little sailboat

CHILDREN LOVE TO sleep on chairs. We sleep in the back room.

There are not enough beds in the shack, which is a stone's throw from the fishermen's cooperative. My mother uses three chairs to make a bed. She turns one around so that the seat is towards the wall. The second she positions the other way round, in other words with its back to the wall, and the third, like the first, with the seat towards the wall. This means that you aren't likely to fall and you can sleep until dawn, before the boats come in. My father and mother sleep in the big bed; my sister curls up in a corner with a rag doll.

My uncle has heaved a mattress onto the kitchen table in order,

—

he says, to avoid scorpions. He sleeps there between the window and the door, just to the left of a flypaper dangling from the ceiling. My father told him to make sure not to get his hairs – his little fly and all his stuff – stuck to it. This aroused raucous laughter in the shack. I myself did not understand the remark. Nor did I ask for a translation. For me words are like flies escaping from the lips. Words stick to things, and words with no place to land end up with the others on the flypaper dangling so close to my uncle's endangered knees. I think you have to catch words in order to invent things. Flies escaping from the flypaper are so many things in embryo that come to life for me all day long, there behind the fishermen's cooperative.

Our shack, surrounded by reeds and built on pilings, is cluttered with spare lumber, sheets of tarpaper, egg cartons, galvanized iron, and cardboard. Two large tires holding geraniums flank the gate in the fence.

There are two rooms in the shack. A radio set, a table, and straw chairs. A gas ring balanced on cinderblocks heats fish soup by the window. Three photos on the radio and a calendar are like eyes in the wall.

There is a dog in the house and a cat. The two of them sleep together by the door. The dog comes into the bedroom every morning and licks our faces to wake us up.

At the entrance a curtain of metal bottle tops waves back and forth. It ripples and jingles like small change when the *tramuntana* blows.

I am walking to the sea for the first time. Riffling the reeds and the airy scrub, the birds arouse the trees also. A man gives me his hand. Shadows shift ahead of us and catch up with us relentlessly in the pale light. Like a dog I am afraid of my shadow and I turn to bite it.

My father squeezes my hand more and more tightly. Suddenly we breathe in the smell of sardines and see the sun coming up behind the boats. We hear the sea. In fact we have been hearing it for a long time, but now its roar comes in full force.

I let go of my father's hand and run off towards its noise and color. Then my father starts shouting:

"Stop! Come back!"

My father grabs my arm just as I am about to touch the froth spreading over the sand.

"Don't touch the sea."

Then he picks me up and holds me in his arms to watch the sea coming towards us.

Without realizing it we are contemplating something beyond the sea. An old rag. An island. No boats. No birds. All we really hear now is the sound of the foam on the sand. Saliva gathers in my throat as my father puts me down beside him on the sand. I feel the endless backwash of the sea between my toes.

—

My father kneels down next to me. He clasps my hands between his and slowly begins to talk to himself. I don't understand right away what he is saying:

"We were two thousand."

Then he repeats: "We were two thousand surrounded by barbed wire."

I hear breathing. His, both of ours, and then that of something breathing beneath the sand. My father takes me by the shoulders, turns me towards him and tells me:

"This is where the soldiers guarded us, mounted on horseback."

I understand the words. Barbed wire I have seen at the entrance to the village. And I know what soldiers are. I have seen soldiers. I know what two thousand means. Two times a thousand is a lot of men. Two thousand is all the birds, all the dogs, all the trees. Two thousand birds, two thousand dogs. But I do not know two thousand men. I know only my father who is just one man, born somewhere in a town in Spain, on Victor Praderas Street, behind a railroad station.

My father cups up sand with his hands.

"Just here a soldier went right into the sea on his horse."

And again: "We were two thousand in that camp."

The sun, like an egg yolk, has risen completely from the sea. The froth kissing our feet has begun to spit at our thighs. The yellow is turning redder on the horizon. The air is separating from the water and birds are being born in the air and don't yet know how to fly.

My father says: "Listen, we'll hear the sea..."

Seashells are the broken bones of men. I collect what belongs to me of death against death and I see doors on the sea that you open with women's hair. I also see men pushing mirrors into the sea for the sea to admire its reflection in a Sunday way.

Seashells are the sun's milk teeth that it leaves to the world every evening as it dies. All day long I am as old as the sun. I pick up a shell and listen to it to see if it is stronger than the sea.

I say to my father: "I've heard another sea."

The shell hears the sea and understands the world's secret things. The shell is also an ear ripped from the sun. This shell was here when my father was two thousand. And this bird. And this dog barking behind him. This sawtooth butterfly too, batting its wings on a rusty tin can.

A little higher now, the sun is an even redder egg yolk in the sky. I see a boat go past. Then two boats. The blue gets to be very far off over the sea.

"We were naked and the soldiers brought us here to shit – we had the runs."

I know what the runs are. I had a stomach ache and it lasted quite a few days.

—

"This beach was our shithouse, and it was the sea that wiped our asses. Think of it: two thousand asses guarded by soldiers!"

I look at the sea that I can hear in the shell. I also hear words from the shack, the ones that escaped from the flypaper and turned into things for me like the words of the sea and the things of death.

In the shell I suddenly see a naked man squatting in the sea. I also see a soldier and then carts loaded with those who have died in the night. And then, too, other men squatting in the sea and more soldiers.

I go for a swim in the sea. Tomorrow too I'll go for a swim. Swimming for three days in a row.

And then the sea falls into its trough of white feathers. The sea sinks deep into the sea. Sinks deep into the bird. Deep into the sky. I watch it digging a tunnel into the light.

I have been swimming three times.

Later I say to my mother in the cabin:

"My father, he was two thousand and shitting in the sea, guarded by soldiers."

And my mother says to my father:

"What have you been telling this child?"

And my father replies:

"Nothing. I told him nothing."

Several seas later. Twenty seas later, I return. Twenty years on.

There is no man beside me as I listen to the beach. Behind me are two thousand ghosts holding berets being marched along by soldiers. I step over bodies, radios, white chairs, and sandcastles. Beach towels have slipped off the bodies and dark glasses are heaped up on the sand like the skeletons of eyes that have never seen anything.

I bump into ghosts of the soldiers and the severed hooves of their horses. Amidst abandoned flags and pants I contemplate an old photograph on an umbrella handle.

I picture my father's coffin descending into Terre-Cabade Cemetery in Toulouse. Now I am older than him, and it occurs to me that since he died I have grown old enough to be his father.

My father, under heaven, gave me the finest shithouse in the world. Hope has its cesspools just as despair does, and the sea is beautiful before me. The saliva of that blue beast continues to lick at my legs.

The shack my uncle knocked together behind the ice cream man a hundred meters from the camp is no longer there, nor are my aunt's red geraniums, nor the three chairs my mother set up every night as a bed. But I hear a kid running around the shack and the tinkling of the curtain of twisted bottle tops the cat used to play with. The windmill in the sky no longer generates the power to light the bulb in the kitchen.

I think of the dozens of words dead on the flypaper above the

———

table, and then of all those that escaped to create things for us and against us.

I look at the sea once again. I want to pull it up over the land like a flag. And I think that a flag made of water would flood the whole earth and drown all the people. And that this would be good for the earth and for the people.

Two birds are whistling back and forth and a file of women are carrying baskets of fish on their heads. The sea will never be a flag and I am proud of the sea.

I recognize the yellow yolk of the sun trembling in the clouds. The same one I saw for the first time all those seas ago. I know that it will give birth to a white bird.

My shadow sinks into my shadow and the sea sinks into the sea. Everything is in order. The sky tunnels through the light.

I turn and call my father in a low voice because that is how you are supposed to call the dead:

"Compañero... Compañero..."

Playfully I throw his black beret between two gulls that are squabbling over the center of the sun as though its glare was carrion.

I walk in the direction of the border, shoes slung over my shoulder, because nothing is yet finished and I still have work to do on the other side of the mountains.

Suddenly a third gull appears with the cry of a woman in labor and the sun begins to stir the wind. An unseen sky swallows itself in little sips of light.

archipelago books

is a not-for-profit literary press devoted to
promoting cross-cultural exchange through innovative
classic and contemporary international literature
www.archipelagobooks.org